Copyright Notice

ISBN: 978-1-953668-17-2

Author's Note

    This book has been *years* in the making—and I mean that. The idea first took shape toward the end of 2023, but inspiration refused to settle. Life decided to show up full force and took what little creative energy I had left.

    My last release was in November of 2020, and now here we are in early 2026 with MARKED. I know this story won't be everyone's cup of tea, and it does address sensitive and difficult topics. Still, I ask that you read it with an open mind and an open heart.

    As always, I'd love to hear your thoughts—your feedback and reviews truly mean more than you know.

    Be YOU-tiful, and never let anyone tell you the sky's the limit when there are already footprints on the moon.

Dedication

Thank you for supporting me in this journey. I greatly appreciate your love and support, as it is what motivates me. Many things inspired me to write this piece, including the need to release another work to satisfy you all, my fans.

I would like to take a moment to thank my family and friends for their consistent words of motivation, as they also play a significant role in keeping me moving forward. As you read this new piece, I ask that you read it, as though you've never known who B.M. Gage is; as though you've never heard my voice before; as though you've never listened to my show and have NO IDEA how I think. Read it with a new mind; if you don't know who I am, that's even better! All I ask is that you learn more about me by visiting my website & following my socials:

> Website: https://bmgage.com
> Facebook - https://facebook.com/officialbmgage
> X - https://x.com/officialbmgage
> Instagram - https://instagram.com/officialbmgage
> TikTok - https://tiktok.com/officialbmgage

Special thanks to Y.B. Redencion for the translations in this piece. This piece wouldn't have the same impact if it weren't for your support and assistance.

1

"I want this entire scene checked thoroughly," Celeste said. Her voice was tight—sharper than she intended—but she didn't apologize. The overhead kitchen light cast a sterile glow across her tired eyes, highlighting the strain she'd carried from one crime scene to the next. "This is the third case in the past month."

The words hung there, heavy, like dust that refused to settle.

Uniformed officers moved quietly around her, careful not to disturb anything they didn't have to. Evidence markers dotted the floor like tiny yellow flags of surrender. The low murmur of radios and quiet footsteps filled the house, but underneath it all was something louder—

The absence of a child.

She looked toward the parents—two silhouettes frozen in fear near the kitchen table, hollowed by shock. They weren't really seeing the officers, the notepads, the gloves. They were staring through everything, as if Christine might reappear if they just willed reality to bend.

"Make sure you gather every piece of information you can from them," Celeste added, her tone leaving no room for argument.

She turned away before the pain in the parents' eyes could settle too deeply. Moving toward the kitchen island, Celeste pulled out her phone. Her hand trembled—barely, but enough that she noticed and silently cursed her own body for betraying her.

Taking photos of crime scenes was all too familiar, muscle memory at this point. She'd done it in apartments littered with drugs, in alleys stained with blood, and in houses where violence had carved its way through families.

Yet tonight, each click seemed louder.
Each flash seemed harsher.
Each image felt like a piece of a puzzle that refused to take shape.

This house wasn't chaotic. It was chillingly normal.

No forced entry.
No triggered alarm.
No overturned furniture.

The sink was clean: a sponge resting on a small ceramic tray; a pink plastic cup, ringed with faint cartoon unicorns, sat drying upside down; a school flyer was magneted to the refrigerator, announcing a "Family Fun Night" in cheerful colors; Christine's name was circled in purple marker near the bottom.

Just a quiet home that hours ago held a living, laughing child, now held a suffocating silence.

Celeste's gaze drifted to the back of the kitchen. The unlocked window immediately caught her attention.

It sat there, slightly ajar, the curtains shifting faintly with the night breeze.

Mocking her.
Accusing her.
Daring her to find what she'd missed.

She stepped closer, careful not to touch the sill. Cool air brushed her skin, carrying the faint scent of damp earth and desert dust. From somewhere beyond the house came the low hum of traffic, a tire rolling over gravel—small reminders that the world kept moving, unaware of what had unfolded here.

At her back stood members of her team: Detective Eternity Smith, Inspector Kristian Hudson, and Officer Candace Kingston.

But everything had changed.

Celeste Carter had served with the Las Vegas Police Department for years—long enough to rise to Deputy, long enough to lead a team of eight: Detective Lucinda Yates, Officer Sebastian Ortega, Detective Maria Suarez, Officer Rita Gaines, Detective Alfred Drummond, Inspector Kristian Hudson, Officer Candace Kingston, and Detective Eternity Smith. Long enough to think she understood darkness in all its shapes: the kind born from greed, from desperation, from rage.

But this—children vanishing without a sound, plucked from their beds like they were nothing—this was a new kind of darkness.

Eternity stood with the parents near the table, her voice soft but steady. She had a notepad in hand, pen poised but still, giving the Hollands space to breathe between questions. As Celeste approached, Eternity finished the introduction.

"Deputy Carter, this is Nico and Leticia Holland. Christine's parents."

Up close, the exhaustion on their faces was almost physical. Leticia's eyes were swollen and red, the skin around them raw from rubbing. Nico looked washed out, like someone had drained the color from his life.

"Good evening, Mr. and Mrs. Holland," Celeste said gently.

Leticia's shoulders shook as silent sobs racked her small frame. Her hands hid her face as if she could block out reality with sheer will. Nico stepped forward—almost automatically, like his body moved because his mind couldn't— and gripped Celeste's hand.

His fingers were cold. Desperate. Pleading.

No words came out of him, but Celeste didn't need them. She could feel everything he wanted to say tightening in his grip.

"We will work around the clock to find your daughter," Celeste said. She leaned closer so he would hear her clearly— so that the words would cut through the fog. "But we need full cooperation from both of you. The faster we move, the better chance we have at finding Christine."

Nico swallowed hard. His jaw trembled as he nodded, clinging to her words like a lifeline. The kind of grief sitting behind his eyes was the kind that hollowed a person out, slowly and completely.

He whispered. "Whatever you need."

Celeste glanced toward Leticia, whose body shook with each breath. Eternity placed a light hand on the woman's arm, trying to anchor her.

"When scanning the home," Celeste continued, forcing herself to stay in investigative mode, "I noticed your alarm wasn't tripped, and there were no signs of forced entry. But one of your windows was unlocked." She deliberately softened her tone. "I know Detective Smith went over this with you. Can you walk me through your evening again?"

Nico exhaled shakily, eyes unfocusing as he replayed the time before everything shattered.

"We got home from Christine's gymnastics class," he began. "She talked the whole way about how her coach said she was improving. She... she wanted to show us her cartwheel again after dinner." His lips quivered around the memory. "We ate. She showered. Put on her pajamas. We read her a story. She got ready for bed. Everything was... normal."

His voice cracked, the last word breaking apart.

"Then my wife checked on her." He looked helplessly at Leticia. "And she was just... gone."

The word echoed through the kitchen like a gunshot.

Leticia's fractured sob cut through the room like a blade. She folded in on herself, elbows on her knees, fingers digging into her hair as if she might be able to reverse time.

Eternity murmured something soothing, but even she looked shaken.

"Did you have anyone over?" Celeste asked, trying to keep her tone calm, factual. It felt cruel to push when they were breaking, but time was their enemy.

"We had friends over earlier," Leticia whispered through her hands. "Omar and Lisette Aguilar. They came to congratulate Christine on making the team..."

Her voice faded like a signal losing strength.

Celeste nodded. "Do you have their number?"

Nico kissed his wife's forehead, lingering there for a second like he didn't want to let go. Then he pulled back and headed upstairs. Each step he took echoed through the quiet house like a countdown clock Celeste couldn't see.

Leticia sank onto a barstool, her voice barely audible. "I just... I don't understand. Who would want to take our little girl?"

Celeste rested a steady hand on the counter beside her, wishing she could offer more than promises and procedure. "We're going to get to the bottom of this," she said. It wasn't enough, but it was all she had.

When Nico returned with the number, his hand shook as he handed the paper over. Eternity wrote it down carefully, then tucked it into a plastic sleeve.

Celeste turned toward the forensics team, forcing herself to detach again.

"What you got?" she asked, crossing the room.

The specialist—a man in his forties with tired eyes and a smudge of black powder on his cheek—held up a strip with partial prints. "These were on the window," he said. "Could be anyone in the house. No smears, no obvious glove marks. No signs of disturbance at all. Floor's clean. Nothing knocked over. No fibers out of place that don't belong."

Celeste looked at the strip, the faint ridges barely visible under the overhead light. The window behind him sat innocently in its frame.

"We'll run them anyway," she murmured.

The specialist nodded. "Parents are shaken," he added quietly, glancing over at Nico and Leticia. "More than usual."

"Third abduction in a month," Celeste whispered, mostly to herself. "And they're all following a pattern... This is bigger than a simple kidnapping."

She stared at the window for a long moment.

Whoever had come through it—or opened it, or used it as a prop—had moved like smoke. No broken glass. No muddy footprints. No prints that screamed stranger. Just enough to say someone had been there.

Just enough to taunt her.

***

"Last night, a seven-year-old girl was abducted from her home around 10:30 p.m."

Celeste pinned Christine's photo to the board, pressing the thumbtack into the cork with more force than necessary. The fluorescent lights in the briefing room hummed overhead. The smell of burnt coffee and dry-erase markers lingered in the air.

The gesture twisted something deep in her chest. Pinning children onto a display always felt wrong—like she was labeling them, cataloging them, turning their lives into exhibits for an investigation.

Rita sat with her arms crossed, leg bouncing rapidly, the rhythmic tap of her heel betraying more anxiety than her expression did. "Third abduction in a month," she said, shaking her head. "Think they're connected?"

"All abductions follow the same pattern," Eternity said, flipping through her notes with quick, anxious fingers. "Young girls. All in athletic activities—gymnastics, soccer, cheer. No alarms tripped. No forced entry. No obvious struggle at the scene."

"Someone they know?" Sebastian asked, leaning forward, elbows on the table.

"Possibly," Eternity said. "But what's the motive? No ransom notes. No communication. No demands."

Celeste stared at the board—Christine Holland, Sonya Friedman, Estelle Gray. Three innocent faces. Three bright futures stolen. Someone was out there hand-picking little girls, slipping into their homes without a trace, leaving behind nothing but questions and parents breaking apart at the seams.

"Beautiful little girls..." Celeste whispered. Her throat tightened as a tear escaped despite her efforts. She blinked it away quickly, but everyone in the room respected her too much to pretend they hadn't seen it.

She thought of her six-year-old niece—wild curls that never stayed in a ponytail, a gap-toothed smile that made every room feel lighter, the way she giggled at the simplest jokes.

If anyone ever took her—She'd burn the world down.

Wiping her eyes quickly, Celeste regained her composure. Straightening her composure, the deputy returned to the front of the room.

"Team, we've got to get to the bottom of this," she said, voice firm again. "We're not letting a fourth girl hit this board."

"We got you," Kristian said from the far side of the table. He straightened in his seat; eyes locked on the photos like he was memorizing every detail.

Celeste nodded. "Check with your C.I.s. Split into teams. Some of you work Sonya's case; others work Estelle's. Compare everything. Every detail. I'm going to Christine's circle again—family, friends, neighbors. If this is the same network, they're evolving."

"I got a C.I. tied to a crew that moves heavy product through West Vegas," Alfred said, already reaching for his badge and keys. "They hear things. I can ask around."

"Good," Celeste replied. She pointed as she spoke, assigning roles with practiced efficiency. "Take Eternity and Sebastian with you. Candace, come with me. Lucinda, Kristian—visit Sonya's family. Rita, Maria—check in with

Estelle's people. Look for overlap. Names, vehicles, places. Anything that repeats."

Her team nodded. A silent pact passed through the room—unspoken but understood. They gathered their gear, chairs scraping back, papers rustling, and the low hum of determination replacing the earlier tension.

As they moved out, Celeste stayed behind for a few seconds. Alone with the board.

She stepped closer to Christine's photo, letting herself feel the weight of it. The tiny sticker on the corner—stuck on by some previous officer to code the case file number—felt obscene near the child's smiling face.

"Hang on, kiddo," she whispered under her breath. "We're coming."

She turned and followed her team.

The sky had shifted to a bleached blue by the time Celeste and Candace stepped outside the station. The sun was high but weak, fighting its way through a layer of hazy cloud that made everything look washed out. Heat rose from the pavement, warping the air slightly.

Celeste dialed Omar's number as they walked to the cruiser.

"Hello?" His voice on the other end was tense, clipped.

"Mr. Aguilar, this is Deputy Carter. We spoke last night regarding Christine."

There was a beat of silence—a heartbeat, maybe two. "Yes," he said finally. "I remember. Did you find her?"

"Not exactly," Celeste replied. "I'd like to speak with you and your wife again."

Another pause. Longer this time. Celeste could almost hear the shift in his breathing, the quiet scramble of thoughts.

"We're home," he said quietly. "But I don't know what more we can offer."

"We just need clarity on a few things," Celeste said. She kept her tone neutral, professional. Beside her, Candace watched her closely, reading not just Omar's words, but the spaces between them.

Omar sighed—a weary, resigned sound. "Fine."

"We'll be there in ten minutes."

When the line disconnected, Candace raised a brow as they reached the car. "He sounds nervous."

"He does," Celeste agreed, unlocking the cruiser. "Let's get to it before they change their mind."

They drove in near silence, the hum of the engine filling the gaps between their thoughts. The suburban streets leading to the Aguilar home looked like any other family neighborhood—trees lining the sidewalks, chalk drawings fading on driveways, bikes tossed on lawns. It was the kind of place that was meant to feel safe.

It didn't.

"Think they're involved?" Candace asked finally, keeping her gaze on the road ahead.

"I think they know something," Celeste said. "Whether they're involved or just scared… that's what we're here to figure out."

They arrived quickly. The Aguilars' house looked pristine from the outside—white stucco, manicured lawn, a small potted plant on the doorstep. No sign of chaos. No sign that anything was wrong.

Candace knocked, and Omar opened the door almost immediately—too fast, as if he'd been standing right behind it, listening for the knock.

His eyes darted between them for a second before he forced a smile that didn't reach his eyes.

"Mr. Aguilar, this is my partner, Officer Kingston," Celeste said.

"Good morning," he replied, stepping aside to let them in. "Lisette should be down soon."

The house felt tense—too quiet, too controlled—no television on in the background. No music. No distant sound of kids playing in their rooms. Just stillness.

They sat on the couch in the living room. The furniture was neat, almost staged. A family photo on the wall showed Omar and Lisette with Cynthia and Luis at a park: all smiles, sunshine catching in the children's hair. In the photo, they appeared to be the typical family.

Now, Omar's hands couldn't seem to find a place to rest. He rubbed his palms on his jeans, then clasped them, then folded them, then unfolded them again. Celeste noticed each movement and took a mental note.

Lisette came down the stairs moments later, smoothing her hair as she joined the others. She wore a soft blouse and jeans, the kind of casual outfit that suggested she was calm, even if everything about her posture said otherwise.

"When you left the Hollands' home last night, how were things?" Celeste asked.

"Everything was normal," Omar said. "We talked about school starting, carpooling. You know, the usual stuff that parents with kids in extracurriculars talk about."

Celeste nodded slowly. "How many children do you have?"

"Two," Lisette said. "Cynthia and Luis. They're close in age to Christine."

"Where are they now?" Candace asked.

"Upstairs," Omar said quickly. "We told them to stay quiet."

"If you don't mind," Celeste said, "we'd like to speak with them. Sometimes, children notice things adults overlook."

Another nervous look passed between Omar and Lisette, a flicker of something unspoken—but they nodded.

"Cynthia, Luis, *bajen las escaleras por favor*," Omar called.
(Cynthia, Luis, come downstairs please.)

Small footsteps padded down the stairs. Two children appeared at the edge of the hallway, eyes wide and cautious.

"Deputy Carter and Officer Kingston are police officers," Lisette said gently. "They want to talk to you about Christine."

"Did you find her?" Cynthia asked, hope flaring in her face like a sudden light.

Celeste's heart squeezed. She wanted to say yes so badly. Instead, she knelt slightly to meet the girl's eye level.

"Not yet, sweetheart," she said softly. "But we're trying. We're working very hard to bring her home. When was the last time you saw her?"

"Yesterday," Cynthia said. "Before flipping class. She was happy."

There was a faint tremble in her voice, but she spoke clearly. Brave.

Celeste nodded. "You're very brave. And Christine is lucky to have a friend who cares about her."

But as she spoke, Cynthia's eyes flicked toward her parents—just a twitch, barely there.

Enough to send Celeste's instincts humming.

Something was off—very off.

Cynthia watched her mother the way some adults watched judges: carefully. Measuring what was allowed.

Kids that age didn't do that unless they'd been told— explicitly or implicitly—to be careful.

"And after flipping class," Celeste asked gently, "did you see Christine again?"

Cynthia hesitated. Her gaze shifted, this time toward her father. A tiny movement, but it might as well have been a siren.

Omar leaned forward. "The girls were tired," he said. "They went to bed early."

It was supposed to sound casual. It didn't. His words landed too fast, too eager to plug the gap.

Celeste shot Candace a subtle look. Candace's eyebrow lifted a fraction in response—enough for Celeste to know they were reading this the same way.

"Cynthia," Candace said softly, "you're helping us by talking. You're doing great."

Luis suddenly spoke, his voice sharper than expected for someone his size. "Are you gonna take us too?"

Lisette inhaled sharply through her nose—barely audible, but Celeste caught it.

Candace gave Celeste a look to ask why Luis said 'too'.

'They're scared. Defensive. Not of us—but of something being revealed.'

"We're here to keep you safe," Celeste said gently. "Not to take you anywhere, okay? We're just asking questions."

Luis didn't look convinced. He moved closer to his sister, shoulder brushing hers, small hand fisting the hem of her shirt.

Candace leaned forward with a small, reassuring smile. "You two play with Christine a lot, right?"

They both nodded.

"Did she say anything yesterday?" Candace continued. "Anything at all that seemed different? About her day, about anyone she met, anything she was worried about?"

A pause. Another.

Cynthia's lower lip trembled. She opened her mouth—

—and Lisette placed a hand on her shoulder. Soft. Gentle. But firm enough that Cynthia's words died in her throat.

Celeste's eyes narrowed slightly. A warning disguised as comfort.

Cynthia swallowed hard. "No… nothing different."

A lie.

Not a malicious one. A forced one. Hesitant. Frightened. Wrapped in the understanding that telling the truth would hurt someone, somewhere.

Omar cleared his throat. "Are we almost done? The kids have schoolwork."

He desperately wanted the conversation to end.

Celeste remained outwardly calm. "Just one or two more minutes," she said. Her voice didn't change, but her awareness sharpened. "Did Christine mention anyone new?" Celeste asked casually. "Anyone from gymnastics? Any adults she talked about? Maybe someone who gave her something? A coach, another parent, a neighbor?"

A too-quick exchange of glances between Omar and Lisette.

"No," Omar said quickly.

"No one," Lisette echoed, matching his speed.

Celeste and Candace could tell they were lying.
The only question was whether they were lying for self-preservation. Or out of fear of someone else.

"Thank you, kids," Celeste said gently, turning back to Cynthia and Luis. "You were very brave to talk to us."

Cynthia lingered for a moment. Her fingers twisted together, knuckles whitening. She looked as if she were gathering the courage to speak again—to finally say the thing her parents didn't want her to say.

Her eyes lifted to Celeste's. Help, they seemed to say. But then she glanced at her mother.

Whatever courage she'd gathered deflated from her shoulders. Her gaze dropped to the floor.

"*Suban arriba*," Lisette said softly.
(Go on upstairs.)

The children obeyed, small feet retreating up the staircase. The sound faded, leaving the house swallowed in thick, uncomfortable silence.

Celeste straightened, her posture shifting almost imperceptibly. The gentle edges of her tone hardened, not into cruelty, but into authority honed by years of seeing people lie to her.

"Mr. and Mrs. Aguilar," she said, "if there's anything—anything at all—you haven't told us, now is the time. Christine's life may depend on it."

Omar swallowed. "We told you everything."

Another lie.
Celeste felt it—deep and certain, the way she'd learned to feel the difference between fear and deception.

Candace shifted beside her, mirroring the tension, eyes sharp.

"We'll be in touch," Celeste said, rising.

Relief washed over the Aguilars' faces.

Not the reaction of innocent people desperate to find a missing child. Innocent people usually grasped for detectives as they left, begged them to stay, and asked what else they could do.

The Aguilars just looked like they wanted the door closed.

Outside, the hot desert air hit Celeste like a wall. It smelled faintly of asphalt and faintly of dust, the heat radiating from the concrete in shimmering waves.

Candace closed the door behind them with a soft click. "They're hiding something," she said quietly.

Celeste nodded, her jaw tight. "Yeah. And whatever it is… it scares them more than we do."

"Did you hear Luis ask if we were going to take them *too*? Like, why would he ask that?"

"It makes you wonder what the parents aren't telling us."

They walked toward the car. The neighborhood felt less friendly now, less safe. Every closed curtain looked suspicious. Every parked car felt like a potential lookout.

Christine's photo flashed into Celeste's mind, her smile frozen in place on the board back at the station.

'Hang on, baby girl. I'm coming.'

She unlocked the car and slid into the driver's seat, gripping the steering wheel for a long second before starting the engine.

"They know more," she whispered, more to herself than anyone else. "And we're going to find out what."

2

The conference room felt colder than usual when Celeste walked in.

The overhead fluorescent lights cast everything in a harsh, tired white that seemed to leech the color out of the room. A muted hum buzzed from the vents overhead, barely masking the low murmur of keyboards and the rustle of paper. The blinds on the far wall were half-closed, cutting the outside world into thin slats of late-afternoon light.

Her team was already scattered around the long table—files open, laptops glowing faintly, coffee cups resting in various stages of abandonment. Some had rings of dried coffee clinging to the inside. Others sat untouched, the liquid now cold and oily.

Everyone looked exhausted, worn at the edges. Eyes red-rimmed, shoulders slumped, movements slower than usual. They carried the weight of the families they'd spoken to— voices echoing in their heads, faces burned into their memories. The kind of weight that didn't disappear after a shift. The kind that followed you home, sat at your kitchen table, and laid beside you at night.

Celeste paused for a heartbeat in the doorway, letting herself take it in. Her team. Her people. They were as beat up by this as she was.

Then she forced herself forward and took her seat at the head of the table.

"Alright," she said quietly. "Tell me what we've got."

Her voice didn't need to be loud. Every set of eyes in the room was already on her.

Rita exchanged a somber look with Maria before speaking. Her fingers toyed unconsciously with the edge of a file, bending it back and forth.

"Estelle's mom is unraveling," Rita said softly. "She kept insisting Estelle wouldn't run away. Said she'd never leave home voluntarily. Not even for a night. She kept repeating it, over and over, like if she said it enough, it would undo what happened."

Maria nodded, flipping through her notes but not really needing to look. The details were already burned into her mind. "Her *abuela* was there too," she added. "She held onto Estelle's rosary the whole time. Wouldn't put it down, not once. She said she's been praying every night for *una señal… cualquier cosa*. A sign. Anything."

A small ache pressed behind Celeste's ribs. She could picture it so clearly—a grandmother's knuckles around a rosary, lips moving silently, eyes fixed on a door that didn't open.

Rita continued, "The mother said the night Estelle vanished felt… wrong. Too quiet. Like the atmosphere shifted." Rita's eyes flicked up briefly, and Celeste could see that wrongness still clinging to her. "She thought she heard a car door outside but convinced herself it was nothing. She said she didn't want to wake her husband over 'paranoia.'"

"What about their neighborhood?" Eternity asked, her tone clipped and controlled. She had her arms folded, pen held between her fingers like a small baton.

Maria flipped a page. "A neighbor saw a dark sedan cruising the block multiple times in the days before Estelle disappeared. Same car. No front plates. He said it creeped him out, but he never called it in."

Celeste's jaw tightened. "And they didn't think that was worth reporting?"

Maria sighed. "They didn't want to seem paranoid," she repeated. "They kept saying, 'We didn't want to bother anyone. We thought we'd look crazy.'"

Celeste shut her eyes briefly. These families are scared. Not just scared of losing their kids—they were scared to speak, scared to assume, to trust each other, to trust their instincts. Scared to trust them—the very people who were trying to save their children.

A moment of silence passed, heavy as concrete.

Kristian cleared his throat and broke it. "Sonya's parents... something is deeply off," he said, voice low.

Lucinda leaned forward, elbows resting on the table, eyes dark with concern. "Her father claimed they 'monitor' her closely. That they know all her friends, where she goes, what she posts. But when we asked for online accounts or messages, he froze. Like he was terrified we'd find something."

"Afraid for her," Rita asked slowly, "or for them?"

Lucinda hesitated, choosing her words. "That's the disturbing part. It didn't feel like he was trying to protect her privacy. It felt like he was trying to protect... something else. Maybe himself. Maybe the family. Maybe a secret."

Kristian nodded grimly. "Her little brother tried to speak up—twice. Once, when we asked about her friends. Then, when we mentioned her staying late with her study group. Both times, the father put a hand on his shoulder. Firm. Like a warning. And the boy shut down," Kristian scoffed. "The kid wouldn't look at us anymore."

Celeste felt her stomach twist. "He intimidated him," she said.

"Absolutely," Kristian replied. "You could see it in the kid's body language. The second that hand landed, he just… collapsed into himself."

"And Sonya?" Celeste pressed.

Lucinda checked her notes even though she didn't really need to. "She'd been scared for weeks. Sleeping with her light on. Refusing to walk alone if she didn't have to. Her mom said Sonya woke her one night, saying someone was watching her through the window."

"Which window?" Celeste asked.

Kristian pointed to an imaginary layout on the table. "Backyard window. The one that faces the wooded area connected to the East Valley trails."

Celeste exhaled slowly, the breath feeling thick in her chest. A hunting ground. Covered by trees, dimly lit, isolated. Perfect for watching without being seen. Perfect for studying a child's routine.

"Christine's parents are… broken," Candace said suddenly, her voice thinner than usual. She cleared her throat, as if it physically hurt to get the words out. "She's only seven, Carter. Seven."

The reminder struck Celeste like a punch. Christine wasn't some teenager flirting with independence, thinking she knew more than the adults around her. She was seven. A baby, in every way that mattered. Vulnerable in ways teens weren't.

Sebastian added, "They kept apologizing. Over and over. Like they're personally responsible for a criminal's decisions. Her mom said Christine still sleeps with a night-light. Still wants the closet door closed. Said she calls out during nightmares, asking if 'the shadows are gone.'"

Candace nodded, blinking fast. "Her dad admitted Christine had been nervous at bedtime lately. Clingy. Asking to sleep with them more. But he didn't want to 'overreact.' Didn't want to scare her. He kept saying, 'I didn't want to make her feel like there was something to be afraid of.'"

Celeste closed her eyes briefly. They didn't know what they were seeing. They didn't realize their daughter was sensing danger adults were blind to—some predatory presence she couldn't explain. Kids felt that kind of thing. Adults rationalized it away.

"We asked about electronics," Sebastian continued. "They said Christine only uses a tablet for school, but… her dad got jumpy when we asked about recent messages. His pupils blew wide, his jaw tightened. Not guilty—more like ashamed. Or startled that we'd zeroed in on it."

"Think he's hiding something?" Eternity asked.

Sebastian shook his head. "Could be denial. Could be guilt for not paying attention sooner. Could be that she's been getting groomed by someone online and they haven't looked closely enough to notice."

Candace swallowed. "And her mom said Christine had been asking about 'strangers' near the school. People standing by the fence. Cars parked and not moving. But she brushed it off. Told Christine that grown-ups were just waiting for their own kids."

Silence fell over the room. Heavy. Stifling.

Christine wasn't a teen groomed online for months. She was a child.

Which meant whoever took her wasn't just part of the network—they were pushing the limits, crossing boundaries that even other predators didn't cross. Testing the system. Growing bolder.

The stakes weren't just high. They were catastrophic.

Kristian finally spoke, leaning back in his chair and scrubbing a hand down his face. "Something's wrong with the Aguilars," he said. "Those kids almost said more than they meant to. You could feel it. They're scared of their parents."

Candace nodded. "If they aren't hiding something, I'd be shocked. They're either in over their heads or being used as a buffer by someone else."

Celeste rubbed at her temples, tension buzzing beneath her skin like electricity. "They know more," she said. "But whatever has them scared… it's bigger than the Aguilars alone. All the kids seem to be scared of their parents," Celeste wondered aloud.

Eternity leaned back, arms crossed tightly over her chest like she was bracing herself. "We need another angle," she said. "If this network is structured—and it is, it has to be—they're not going to hand us their hierarchy. We're chasing shadows right now."

"Kids are disappearing all over East Valley," Rita said. "Preteens, teens, runaways, grab-and-go kidnaps, online luring. They're using different methods for different targets. It looks chaotic from the outside."

"Chaos isn't random," Celeste murmured. "Not when it repeats in patterns. It's controlled. It's curated."

The team exchanged uneasy glances—fear mingled with dawning clarity, the kind that made your stomach drop because it made too much sense.

Sebastian leaned in, resting his forearms on the table. "Let's say, hypothetically, they're selecting victims based on vulnerability. Girls who blend in. Girls who don't draw attention. Girls who won't fight back hard enough to leave a mark. Girls who look alone."

"Girls who look young," Candace added quietly. "Very young."

And then all eyes shifted to Celeste.

It wasn't dramatic. No gasps. Just eight people who knew her, who trusted her, watching the realization move across her face.

She felt the air change.

The moment a terrible idea is born.

"No," Kristian said instantly, reading her like he always did. "Absolutely the fuck not."

Celeste stood, the legs of her chair scraping against the tile in a jarring sound. "*Piénsalo un segundo. Tiene sentido.* It makes sense."
(Think about it for a second.)

"That's not the point," Rita snapped, her voice sharper than usual. "It's suicide, Carter."

Celeste's voice softened, but it didn't lose its steadiness. It rolled through the room like an anchor line dropping into deep water. "Kids are being taken off streets we patrol. Out of bedrooms their parents tucked them into. Christine is seven—seven. And we're missing something because we're on the outside looking in."

Fear crept around the room, coiling between them, replacing the sterile conference-room chill with an oppressive heat.

"You'd go undercover as a teenager," Candace whispered. "Sixteen? Fifteen?" Her eyes flicked over Celeste's face, assessing, hating that she could actually see it working.

Celeste nodded once.

The silence that followed was suffocating. No one shuffled papers. No one cleared their throat. The only sound was the faint buzz of the lights and the distant rumble of something heavy rolling down a hallway.

Kristian slammed his notebook shut, the sound cracking through the stillness. "You can pass for seventeen. Maybe sixteen on a good day. That's prime target territory for what we're looking at." Defeat could be heard in his words.

Eternity looked like every part of her wanted to reject the idea, but her brain was trained to chase logic. "Predators don't care about birthdays. They care about what someone looks like. Vulnerability is enough. Lonely is enough."

Celeste lifted her chin.

"If this crew targets girls who look alone… then alone is exactly what I need to be."

"And alone is what you'll be," Sebastian murmured. He met her eyes; worry etched deep in his features. "No wire. No team within arm's reach. No cavalry around the corner."

"I have to be," she said. "If any of you tail me, they'll smell it. These guys are cautious. Every scene we've walked into proves that. This is the only way to get inside the ring while it's still forming."

Candace's voice trembled. "They'll grab you like you're nothing," she said. "They'll hurt you, Carter. You know that, right?"

A tremor swept through Celeste—not of fear, but of something harder, sharper. Resolve. The kind of resolve that sat heavy and immovable once it settled.

"If it brings these girls home," she whispered, "I'll take that risk."

The entire room stilled again.

Finally, Kristian swore under his breath. "Then we do this right," he said. "Prep, surveillance, kill-switch, everything. No shortcuts. No cowboy tactics."

"Agreed," Rita said, wiping a tear from the corner of her eye before it could fall. "We're not losing you. We're not putting another face on that board. Not yours."

***

After hours of planning—routes mapped, probable hotspots identified, communication protocols set, what-ifs argued and re-argued until everyone was hoarse—the team gathered once more.

No files this time and no screens.

Just raw fear and fierce loyalty.

They stood in the smaller briefing room now, the one off the main hallway. The lights were dimmer here, the air cooler. It felt more intimate. More like a holding room for decisions no one wanted to make.

Kristian paced like an animal caged in worry, running a hand through his hair repeatedly. "You sure about this?" he asked.

Celeste offered a faint smile. It didn't reach her eyes, but it was real enough. "If I said no," she replied, "you'd think someone already grabbed me."

A few people huffed out soft, broken laughs. It didn't help much, but it was something.

"Celeste," Candace whispered. She was hugging her own arms like she was trying to keep herself from shaking apart. "We can find another angle. We always do. We can flip a CI, push harder on the Aguilars, do something else."

"There isn't one," Celeste murmured. She could feel the truth of it in her bones. "If they're willing to take a child as young s Christine, the whole pattern is shifting. We're running out of time, and they're getting bolder. If we wait, we lose more girls. Maybe forever."

Rita blinked rapidly, her gaze shiny. "Going undercover is one thing," she said. "Getting abducted—intentionally—is something else entirely."

"And you'll be alone," Sebastian reminded her, softer this time, like repeating it might somehow change the outcome.

That truth pressed on Celeste's spine like a heavy hand.

But she lifted her chin. "I need you all to trust me," she said. "Like you always have."

Eternity stepped forward, her expression tight. "If something feels wrong tonight—anything—you pull out," she said. "You don't get to martyr yourself. You don't get to decide your life is worth less than anyone else's. Not on my watch."

Celeste's throat tightened. She'd already decided how she was going to handle the situation, though she didn't share every piece of intel with her team. She looked at each of them—her team, her family in every way except blood. Every face was lined with fear, anger, and stubborn loyalty.

Kristian moved first. He closed the distance between them in two strides and pulled her into a fierce, crushing hug. Celeste stiffened, surprised—physical displays weren't exactly Kristian's style—but then she melted into it, letting her forehead fall against his shoulder.

One by one, the rest joined. Arms wound around her, around each other. An uncoordinated cluster of bodies and emotion. It was messy. Too tight. Half of them were probably stepping on somebody else's boots. But no one moved.

Candace whispered into Celeste's ear, "Come back. Please come back. Don't you dare leave me stuck with these idiots."

Celeste choked out a shaky laugh that sounded dangerously close to a sob. "I'm coming back," she said. "You'll see me complaining in a few days about how nobody can make coffee right."

They stayed in that formation another moment, breathing together, gathering whatever courage they could from shared contact. When they finally pulled away, Celeste felt like something had been left on her shoulders—an invisible mantle made of all their fear and hope.

Sebastian stepped forward with something small in his hand—a braided bracelet, pink, blue, and white threads worn soft from being handled repeatedly.

"From Christine's mom," he said quietly. "She gave it to me after we left. Said it was 'for protection.' Figured you're going to need it more than I do."

Celeste's chest tightened painfully. She took the bracelet reverently, the threads warm from his palm. She tied it around her wrist with trembling fingers, the knot tight.

"I'll bring it back," she whispered.

Out loud, it was a promise. Inside, it was a prayer.

Kristian cleared his throat, voice rough. "We'll be watching," he said. "Even if you can't see us. We won't be far. And the second we get something, anything, we move."

"I know," Celeste murmured.

She turned toward the door, hand brushing the frame for half a second, as if touching the building would root her one last time.

"Let's bring these girls home," she said.

Eight nods answered her. Eight breaking hearts.

And Celeste walked out, feeling the weight of their hope rest heavy—but steady—against her back.

***

The night air tasted metallic as Celeste walked along the cracked sidewalk, like the city itself had turned sour.

The sky above was a deep, bruised purple, the last remnants of daylight swallowed by the urban glow. A lone streetlamp flickered at the corner, its light buzzing and stuttering like it couldn't quite commit. Shadows clung to the edges of buildings, pooling in doorways and alley mouths.

"Talk to me, Carter," Kristian spoke over the radio.
Celeste continued her stride. Staying low, shoulders slightly slumped, and stepping slowly.
"Night four of strolling and nothing as of yet," Kristian added.
"They're watching. They always are," Celeste murmured, barely moving her lips.

Celeste kept her gait uneven, her posture slouched, her expression hollow—exactly the way a lost teenager might appear. Her clothes were deliberately chosen: thrift-store jeans fraying at the hem, scuffed sneakers, and a faded hoodie that was two sizes too big. Her hair was in a single braid that flowed down her back, slightly tangled, face scrubbed of any makeup that might make her look older.

'Stay small. Stay breakable. Stay visible.'

Her instincts buzzed beneath her skin like static. Every hair on her arms felt on alert. Something was wrong. She felt eyes on her—prying, hunting—but nothing moved in her peripheral vision. No obvious tail. No footsteps she could pinpoint.

Just a flickering streetlamp. Distant traffic humming along the bigger roads.

The scrape of her own cheap sneakers on the pavement.

She passed a closed liquor store, its windows gated and tagged with graffiti. A stray cat darted across the road ahead and slipped under a parked car. Somewhere, a dog barked once, then went quiet.

She shifted the strap of her backpack—empty except for a water bottle and a worn-out notebook to complete the illusion. Her fingers brushed the braided bracelet at her wrist.

'Hang on, Christine. Hang on, Sonya. Hang on, Estelle. I'm coming.'

Then—

A shift in the air. So slight she might have missed it if she hadn't been listening for everything.

A soft shuffle behind her. Not the sound of a drunk stumbling, not the uneven rhythm of someone out for a casual walk.

Deliberate. Controlled.

Her heart jolted, slamming once, hard, against her ribs.

'Don't turn. Don't run. Don't break cover.'

She forced her shoulders to hunch even more, letting her arms hang limp. A vulnerable silhouette. A perfect target.

The streetlight above her flickered once—twice—casting the world into brief darkness, then back into dim light.

A shadow spilled across the pavement behind her. It grew, stretching longer, swallowing the smaller outline of her own.

Before she could inhale, an arm hooked around her waist—iron tight, cutting off the air in her lungs. Another hand clamped over her mouth, rough and calloused, the fingers pressing into her cheeks.

Her feet left the ground so fast her stomach lurched. For a split second, the world tilted, the sidewalk spinning away beneath her. A muffled sound—fear mixed with reflex—escaped against the palm, silencing her. It came out high and broken, the perfect sound of a terrified girl rather than a trained cop.

She kicked once, lightly, enough to sell the role. Not enough to cause damage.

"*¡Cállate!*," a harsh whisper hissed against her ear, hot breath ghosting across her skin.
(Shut up!)

A sack dropped over her head, scratchy and suffocating. Rough burlap scraped her face, the fibers catching on her eyelashes. The world went black. Hot. Airless. The smell was overwhelming—sweat, rubber, stale smoke, something chemical and sharp.

Her pulse hammered hard enough to hurt, battering against her temples.

Hands—multiple sets—shifted her weight. She counted them in the chaos of touch and motion. One behind her, arm banded around her middle. Two more at her legs, lifting. Another presence nearby, close enough to feel, not close enough to touch.

Three men. At least.

Her shoulder bumped something hard and cold—metal, the frame of a van door. Then they heaved, and her body slid, half-dropped, into the narrow interior. Her hip hit the floor first, a blunt jolt of pain that flashed up her side.

She sucked air through the burlap, shallow and frantic, the way a terrified captive would. She let her breath stutter; let a small whimper escape.

The door slammed shut behind her with a final, echoing thud.

The engine roared to life, the vibration running up her spine where her back met the van floor. The smell inside intensified—rubber mats, gasoline, something else she didn't want to identify.

Someone yanked her wrists behind her back. Coarse rope bit into her skin as they tied her hands tightly, looped once, twice, a third time for good measure. The knot cinched hard.

A vulnerable girl. Not a cop. Not a threat.

She curled into herself, knees drawn slightly inward, shoulders hunched, making herself smaller. It matched the profile, but it also protected her core.

Her breathing trembled, erratic, perfectly panicked. A thin, wet sound threaded through each inhale. She could hear it. She knew they could, too.

Inside, her mind was razor-sharp.

Her fingers stretched as far as the rope allowed until they brushed against the bracelet on her wrist—the one from Christine's mother. The threads were a small, solid thing in a world that had just gone dark and loud.

A reminder. A promise. She clung to it.

As the van sped away, Celeste listened. She let the external noise fill her, documenting everything.

Three voices. One man close to her smelled like stale cigarettes. His breathing was a little wheezy, like there was something old and burned in his lungs.

Another voice had a thick accent—Latin American, familiar cadence, sharp consonants.

The third was quieter, younger, with shorter words and less certainty.

"Check her pockets," the accented one said in Spanish. *"No teléfono. No nada."*
(No telephone, no nothing.)

Rough hands patted her down, sliding over her hoodie, down her jeans, her ankles. She forced herself not to flinch beyond what a terrified teen would do. They searched quickly and efficiently; clearly practiced.

"Nada," the younger one said. *"No trae celular."*
(Nothing. She doesn't have a phone.)

The route—the van took off with a sharp lurch, tires crunching over loose gravel. Then the surface smoothed out. They made a left at what felt like a shallow angle. A right a few seconds later. She counted seconds in her head.

One, two, three... Turn.
One, two, three, four, five, six... Another turn.

She felt each change in speed, each curve.

Rough road. Potholes. A series of bumps rattled her teeth, likely an older side street or a service road. Then a stretch of smoother asphalt—main road, wider, more maintained. The sound of other cars grew louder, then faded again as they left busier streets.

Industrial zone. Desert edge. Somewhere hidden at the margins.

Celeste hoped that her team witnessed the abduction and the connection was holding out, although she did tell her team that she needed to be alone for this to work and to keep their distance.

The pendant around her neck. Her one chance at communicating with her team. She could feel it resting on her skin.

Celeste took calculated, panicked breaths to sell the role.

"*¿Crees que valga algo?*" the smoker asked in Spanish. "Looks small. Maybe too young."
(You think she's worth anything?)

"Doesn't matter," the accented one replied. "*Hay mercado para todo.* There's a market for everything. And if Pablo says to take them, we take them."

Pablo. Another name to add to the list.

Her heartbeat thundered, but she held herself together. She let herself shake—but not fall apart. There was a difference.

They took the bait.

'Now I find the girls. Now I find the monster behind this.'

The van kept driving. Time stretched, warped by adrenaline. Minutes felt like hours. The darkness inside the sack pressed in, making it hard to tell where her body ended, and the air began.

At one point, the van slowed. Turned. Gravel again. The engine downshifted. The smell of dust thickened. No more city sounds—no distant horns, no layered hum of civilization. Just the engine, the tires, and the low murmur of men.

Finally, the van rolled to a stop.

"*Ya llegamos,*" the accented one said.
(We're here.)

The engine cut off. Silence crashed in, loud and ringing in her ears.

Her wrists throbbed where the rope dug into her skin. Sweat had dried in patches along her spine, leaving her cold and clammy under the hoodie. Her knees ached from the angle she'd been forced to lie in.

A door slid open. Fresh air rushed in—cooler, tinged with dust, faintly metallic. Maybe near warehouses. Maybe near old structures. It didn't smell like the suburbs anymore.

Hands grabbed her under the arms and at her legs again, dragging her toward the open door. Her shoes scraped against the metal floor, then the edge. Then—

Her feet hit rough ground. Hard-packed dirt. Small pebbles bit into the soles.

She stumbled, letting her knees buckle just enough to seem weak, disoriented. One of them jerked her upright with a muttered curse.

"Walk," someone barked.

She did. Blind, hands bound, bag over her head. Each step was careful, toes feeling for obstacles. She could hear their footsteps around her—two close, one slightly ahead, another trailing.

A door creaked open somewhere to her left. Hinges squealed, metal against metal.

She was steered inside. The air changed again— warmer, more confined, scented with old wood, sweat, and something sickly-sweet that turned her stomach.

Another door. Another set of footsteps.

The sack stayed over her head. For now.

She kept walking, heart pounding, mind taking note of everything.

Every voice. Every smell. Every turn. Every piece of the monster's lair she could steal, one sense at a time.

And Celeste—
She had never been more alert.

3

The burlap sack scratched across Celeste's cheeks as rough hands yanked it off her head. The sudden light stung her eyes—red, muted, and eerie, like something breathing through the walls. She blinked hard. Shapes appeared. Voices. A rancid undertone of sweat, mildew, and fear.

She and a few other ladies were crammed inside the back of a car. One of the men pulled her from the vehicle, and Celeste allowed her knees to buckle slightly.

Enrique, the one who smelled of cheap cologne and cigarettes, looked her up and down like she was a product he'd ordered and personally inspected.

"Destiny Rojas," he announced, jerking his chin toward his partner. "Just picked her up tonight."

Celeste let her body shrink in on itself.
Lost. Helpless. Confused—the perfect mask.

Alejandro slid closer, his shadow swallowing hers. "*¿La vendieron?*"
(Was she sold?)

"*No. Es una fugitiva,*" Enrique answered gruffly, grabbing Celeste by the waist. His fingers were cold and uncaring. He smelled like cigarette ash and cheap cologne.
(No. She's a runaway.)

Celeste kept her breathing slow and shallow.
'*You're not Celeste Carter right now. You're seventeen, scared, and alone. Stay small. Stay quiet.*'
Alejandro cupped her face with a hand that felt like ice. He smirked, thumb brushing her cheek. "We're going to have fun with you."
His words were deliberately slow, like he enjoyed watching them sink in.
"*¿Cuántos años tienes?*"
(How old are you?)
Celeste didn't reply. She let her lips tremble.
The slap came fast. Hard. She stumbled sideways and would've fallen if he hadn't fisted a handful of her hair and yanked her upright again.
"Alejandro doesn't like to ask more than once," Enrique muttered.

Alejandro leaned in, lips curling. "*¿Cuántos años tienes?*"
(How old are you?)
His breath was sour. His tone was a threat wrapped in silk.
"*Dies y siete,*" Celeste whispered, voice cracking.
(Seventeen.)
Alejandro's smile widened into something feral.
"*La edad justa. Tan tierna y pura.*"
(The perfect age. So tender and pure.)
He kissed her cheek—a cold, mocking peck.
"You're becoming a woman."
He turned to Enrique. "*Ponla con las demás.*"
(Put her with the others.)
"Which ones?"
"*No importa.*"
(It doesn't matter.)

A brown sack dropped over her face again, swallowing the light. Enrique's hand landed on her shoulder, and he pushed her forward. She heard the van doors creak open, then the crunch of debris under their feet.

And suddenly—
Suddenly, the sensation of being led blind triggered a memory.

———

Jonathan's voice echoed in her head: deep, stern, protective. Jonathan Hernandez was the police commander – one of the few ranks over Celeste.

"If you do this, Carter, you'll be going in blind. The technology isn't there for us to monitor you. These men are more than likely trained to scan for wires, cameras, radio frequencies—anything that could give you away."

Celeste followed him down the hall. She held the missing-children folder tight against her chest, the faces of Christine, Sonya, and Estelle like ghosts staring back.

"Hernandez, if I don't do it, we may never get to the bottom of this. We may never find them. And every hour we delay, more girls disappear."

"Carter—"

"No." She stepped in front of him and placed Christine's necklace on his desk. "We replicate this. Insert a micro-camera in the pendant."

Jonathan's shoulders dropped in exhausted frustration.

"Boss," she pushed, eyes burning, "these are little girls. The oldest one we have record of is fourteen. Our techs have integrated more advanced concepts for drug busts. Don't tell me finding cocaine is worth more to you than finding these girls."

He closed his eyes. "I don't want to put you in harm's way."

"I'm sorry, but I'm putting myself there whether you approve it or not," Celeste said softly. "These girls have already been failed enough. They need someone who won't look away."

Celeste continued the walk with Enrique, and she soon felt a wave of heat hit her arms. The heat washed over her skin as the sack was pulled off. The air was stale and humid, heavy with the scent of old fear.

Celeste blinked.

They were in a boarded-up room—the wood around the windows cracked and splintered. A red lamp glowed in the corner, its bulb flickering like a heartbeat. Shadows clung to the walls.

Girls. At least ten.

All in various states of distress—messy hair, bruises along their arms and legs, some with dried tears staining their cheeks. Their clothes were torn, ill-fitting, or dirty. Many clung to each other like pieces of driftwood in a storm.

Celeste forced the horror down.
'Not now. Focus. Observe.'

"Get over there," Enrique ordered, shoving her forward.

Celeste stumbled into a cluster of girls who instinctively flinched away. Their eyes were wide, haunted, suspicious.

Enrique left, and the door slammed shut, the lock clicking loudly—an iron period to a sentence of captivity.

At first, only whispers stirred in the room. Then the whispers rose into soft, fragile chatter.

A girl stepped forward—a thin, brown-eyed teen with weary strength in her expression. Celeste recognized her immediately.

Angela Sanchez. Missing for three months.

But Celeste forced no recognition, no flicker of relief.
'Play the role. Protect the girls.'

Angela held out a damp towel. "Here," she murmured.

Celeste accepted it with a grateful, trembling smile. "*Gracias.*"
(Thank you.)

Angela softened slightly. "What's your name?"

"Destiny," Celeste answered, wiping her face. "*¿Y tú?*"
(And you.)

"Angela." She glanced at the others. "I… try to look out for everyone here. Gotta stay strong — they need me."

"How old are you?" Celeste asked gently.

"Fourteen." Angela watched her carefully, as if evaluating whether Celeste was trustworthy. "You?"

"Seventeen." Celeste lowered her gaze, mimicking fear. "I was walking to clear my mind, and they kidnapped me. Didn't even get to scream."

Angela's mouth flattened into a sad line.
Softly, she confessed, "Runaway. *Mi papá tiene problemas con el alcohol y ha sido muy abusivo. Varias de estas marcas son por eso.*"
(My dad has problems with alcohol and is very abusive. Several of these marks are from that.)
She showed her arms—faded bruises, some still yellowing.

"*Lo siento,*" Celeste whispered. "*¿Y tu mamá?*"
(I'm sorry. What about your mom?)

Angela shook her head, fingers tangling in her hair. "*No he visto a mi mamá desde que era un bebé.* So… it's always been just my dad."
(I haven't seen my mom since I was a baby.)

Pain and fury tangled in Celeste's gut. These girls deserved better. All of them.

Angela continued in a hushed voice, "Pablo said the older you are, the less pure you are."

"Pablo?" Celeste echoed to get clarification on who he was.

"*Sí.* He's the boss."
(Yes.)

Something cold slid down Celeste's spine.

Angela kept talking, voice trembling despite her attempt to sound strong. "*La más joven que he visto tiene como seis o siete años.*"
(The youngest one I've seen is like six or seven years old.)

Celeste's breath caught.
'Six or seven. God…'

Before she could respond, the door creaked open, and Enrique entered with a bottle of water and a bag of chips.

"Destiny," he said, forcing the items into her hands. "Gotta keep you hydrated. Orders from Alejandro."

He studied her a moment too long. Celeste subtly brushed her hair aside to give the necklace camera a clear line of sight.

He said nothing more, then left.

Celeste leaned closer to Angela. "What about him?"

"Enrique." Angela rolled her eyes, but fear flickered behind it. "He's made several advances to me, *pero* he isn't as aggressive as the others." A tear formed. "Once, he was ordered to 'break me in' and… let's just say he wasn't as forceful as the others have been."

Celeste felt a surge of protective rage so intense she had to clench her jaw to keep it hidden.

"I'm sorry," she murmured. "You don't have to tell me anything that hurts."
Angela shrugged shakily. "*No pasa nada, puedo con eso.*"
(It's okay. I can handle it.)

But her laugh was brittle. Forced.
Celeste looked at the younger girls huddled in the corner and switched exclusively to Spanish.

"*¿Cuántos hombres te han hecho esto?*"
(How many men have done this to you?)

"*En este grupo, tal vez cuatro,*" Angela said. "*Pero siempre nos van pasando de uno a otro.*"
(In this group, maybe four. But they're always passing us off.)

"*¿Cuatro? ¿Todos sexuales?*"
(Four? Are they always sexual?)

Angela nodded. "*Sí, hasta cierto punto.*"
(Yes, to a certain extent.)

Celeste's heart kicked hard against her ribs. If Angela has only encountered four, the network might be larger.

"*¿Y las chicas más jóvenes?*"
(What about the younger girls?)

"*Los cuatro no se meten con niñas menores de once. Supongo que son demasiado inocentes,*" she said with disgust.

(The four here don't mess with any of the girls under eleven. I guess they're too pure.)

Celeste swallowed the smallest drop of relief. Not safe. Just… less targeted.

"*¿Hay más chicas?*"
(Are there more girls?)
"*Hay tres, cuartos más. Más o menos el mismo número.*" Angela pointed to the wall. "*A veces cenamos juntas… o nos reúnen para pasar lista.*"
(About three or four. Roughly about the same amount. Sometimes they gather us together to take roll call or when it's time to eat.)

Celeste's blood went cold. They're organized. Systematic. Confident.

The door opened again. Enrique.
Every girl fell silent. Some closed their eyes. One flinched so violently she nearly toppled over.
Enrique walked slowly. Too slow. His eyes dripped over Celeste like oil.
"You girls seem to be getting along very well," he chuckled. "Don't get any cute ideas," he forcibly tossed a blanket at Celeste.

Celeste forced her shoulders to hunch as she grabbed the sheet, her eyes widening like a frightened doe. "Is it wrong for us to laugh and talk?"
Enrique licked his lips. "You're a feisty one; always got a comeback or something to say. *Me gusta.*"
(I like it.)
He smirked, then turned his attention to another girl nearby.
Celeste held her breath until he left.
Angela leaned close. "*Él…* he's not the worst. But he enjoys the power."

Celeste nodded and forced a small, shaky laugh. Changing topics to lighten the mood— "I need something done to these ends," she muttered, touching her hair. "I was supposed to get them fixed."

Angela blinked, startled by the shift. Then she let out a soft laugh—one with a spark of real life in it.

She reached toward Celeste's hair but hesitated. Celeste nodded permission.

Angela sifted through the strands. "It's not that bad. Let me grab some scissors and oil someday *y te lo arreglo*."

(And I'll take care of it.)

"Oh yeah?" Celeste teased lightly. "And what do you know about doing hair?"

Angela gasped in mock offense. "*¿Estás bromeando?* I used to do my friends' hair all the time. They always said I'd be their beautician when we got older."

(Are you kidding?)

The smile on her face grew, but her voice softened at the end—grief wrapped in nostalgia.

Celeste's heart cracked.

"Well," Celeste whispered, "until we get out of here, you're my full-time beautician. Hook your girl up."

Angela's face lit up.

For a moment—just a moment—the red-lit prison faded. They were two girls talking about hair, about futures they were supposed to have, and about life beyond the walls.

And Celeste made herself a promise:

No matter what it cost her, these girls would walk into the sun again.

■■■

The bullpen felt wrong without Celeste.

Her chair sat empty at the far end of the table, her coffee mug still parked near the edge, a faint ring of dried coffee shadowing its base. Her jacket hung from the rack by the door, as if she'd just stepped out for a lunch break instead of willingly walking into the jaws of a predator.

The team filed back into the conference room in a slow, uneven trickle. No one spoke at first. The whiteboard at the front of the room glowed under the fluorescent lights, the three faces—Christine, Sonya, Estelle—watching them in silent accusation.

Kristian shut the door behind them with a soft but definitive click.

Eternity dropped into a chair and stared at the photos, arms folded, fingers drumming against her biceps. Rita and Maria slid into seats side by side, their notebooks already open, though neither of them reached for a pen. Candace sank into her chair as if her bones hurt. Sebastian remained standing, one hand gripped around the back of his chair, restless energy pulsing through him like he needed to move or punch something.

The air felt too still. The clock on the wall ticked too loudly.

After a moment, Kristian cleared his throat. "Where's Hernandez?" he asked.

"Talking to tech," Sebastian said. "They're still trying to re-establish a feed."

A ripple of tension passed through the room at that. Everyone knew what he meant by feed.

They'd all heard it twenty minutes ago: the steady crackle in their earpieces as the tech team tried to reach Celeste. The repeated calls. The absence of her voice. The moment when the line had gone from weak interference to absolutely nothing.

Celeste had gone under.

And then she'd gone dark.

The door opened, and Jonathan stepped in, looking like he'd aged ten years in the last two hours. The precinct commander's tie was loosened, top button undone, sleeves rolled to his forearms. He carried a tablet under one arm, his jaw working.

Behind him came Malik from tech—mid-thirties, hoodie under a blazer, phone still in his hand like he'd been dragged straight from his workstation.

Celeste's seat at the head of the table was empty.

No one took it.

Hernandez set the tablet on the table and remained standing, hands planted on its metal edge. His gaze swept the room, counting them like he was bracing himself against the fact that one of his people was missing.

"Alright," he said. His voice didn't carry the usual bark of command—it carried something heavier. "Let's start with what we know. Then we'll move to—" he glanced at Celeste's empty seat. He cleared his throat and wiped a tear from the corner of his eye. "What have we got?"

No one missed the pause and the cracking in his voice.

He looked to Rita first. "Estelle."

Rita exchanged a glance with Maria, then set her notebook on the table and opened it, though her eyes never dropped to the page.

"Estelle's mom is unraveling," Rita said quietly. "She's barely sleeping. She kept insisting Estelle wouldn't run away. Said it over and over— 'she wouldn't leave me. She wouldn't leave without saying goodbye.' Like she was arguing with fate."

Maria nodded, fingers laced together on the tabletop. "Her *abuela* was there," she added. "She held onto Estelle's rosary the entire time. Wouldn't let go. Said she's been praying every night for *una señal… cualquier cosa*. A sign. Anything."

A muscle ticked in Kristian's jaw. Candace swallowed hard, her gaze glued to the crime board.

Rita went on. "Her mom said the night Estelle vanished felt… off. Too quiet. No wind, no dogs barking, no cars passing. She said it felt like the whole street was holding its breath." Rita hesitated for a second. "She thought she heard a car door outside sometime after ten. But she told herself it was nothing. She didn't want to 'wake her husband over something stupid.'"

"What about the neighbors?" Eternity asked, voice low.

Maria flipped a page. "One neighbor mentioned a dark sedan cruising the block in the days leading up to the abduction. Same car, no front plates. Slow driving. He said it gave him a bad feeling, but he never wrote down a description or bothered to call it in. He told us, 'I didn't want to be that crazy neighbor.'"

Jonathan's lips pressed into a thin line. He didn't bother to hide his frustration. "They're scared of looking paranoid," he muttered. "So, they say nothing."

"And the right people listen to that silence," Sebastian said quietly.

Jonathan nodded once and shifted his attention. "Kristian, Lucinda -- Sonya."

Kristian leaned forward, elbows on the table, hands clasped so tightly his knuckles had gone white. "Sonya's father is a problem," he said flatly. "He claims he 'monitors' her closely. Says he knows all her friends, where she goes, what she posts. But when we asked for her phone and social accounts, he shut down. Refused to give access. Called it an 'invasion of privacy.'"

Lucinda's jaw clenched. "We told him he could be present while we looked," she said. "We explained we have techs who can limit searches by keyword and timeframe. He still refused. His pulse spiked, his pupils blew wide. That wasn't grief—that was fear."

"Afraid for her," Rita asked, "or for himself?"

Lucinda hesitated. "That's the disturbing part. It didn't feel like he was trying to protect her. It felt like he was trying to keep something buried. Maybe it's unrelated. Maybe he's hiding something else—abuse, conversations, an affair. But whatever it is, he'd rather slow us down than let us see it."

Kristian exhaled slowly. "Her younger brother tried to speak up twice," he added. "Once, when we asked about her friends. Again, when we mentioned her staying late for a study group. Both times, the father put a hand on his shoulder. Firm. And the kid shut down. Shoulders dropped. Eyes on the floor. I've seen that look before."

"He intimidated him," Jonathan said.

"Absolutely," Kristian replied. "That kid's scared of his father. That doesn't mean Dad took her. But it sure as hell means there are secrets in that house."

"And Sonya herself?" Jonathan asked.

Lucinda flipped back a page. "Her mom said she'd been scared lately. Sleeping with her light on. Asking not to walk home alone. She woke her mom up one night, said someone was watching her through the window."

"Which window?" Sebastian asked, even though he knew.

"The one facing the wooded area behind their house," Kristian answered. "The same greenbelt that connects down toward the East Valley industrial strip."

Jonathan grimaced. "Perfect sightlines, no street traffic, easy access in and out," he said. "A stalker's playground."

He turned toward Candace and Sebastian. "Christine."

Candace took a breath that shook more than she wanted it to. Her eyes betrayed all the sleep she hadn't gotten. "Her parents are…" She paused, searching for the word. "Breaking. Her mom can barely get through a sentence without apologizing for something—anything. She keeps saying, 'We should have checked more. We should have known.'"

Sebastian took over, his voice low. "They described Christine as… a little kid. Not a 'tween, not a mature-for-her-age type. Stuffed animals in the bed, unicorn night-light. She asks her mom to check the closet for monsters."

Candace nodded. "Her dad said she'd been more nervous at bedtime lately. Asking to sleep with them more. Jumping at noises. He chalked it up to regular childhood fears. He told me, 'We didn't want to make a big deal out of it. Didn't want her to think there was actually something to be afraid of.'"

"But there was," Eternity said softly.

"We asked about electronics," Sebastian continued. "They said she only used her tablet for schoolwork. Some games. Nothing social. But when I asked if we could see recent messages—or if she'd been using any apps to chat—her dad got… jumpy. Not defensive. Just ashamed, almost. Like he was realizing, in real time, how much he hadn't checked."

"Hiding what?" Jonathan asked.

Sebastian spread his hands. "We don't know yet. They consented to us pulling the tablet. Tech's combing through it now, but nothing obvious has popped yet—no flagged handles, no clear grooming pattern. If there's something there, it's subtle, or buried deep."

Candace swallowed. "Her mom mentioned Christine had started talking about 'strangers near the school,'" she said. "Adults standing outside the fence. Cars parked just across the street that never moved. But she brushed it off, told her they were just waiting for their kids. Or checking their phones."

Silence dropped over them again.

Seven years old. Still afraid of closet monsters.
And she'd been right to be afraid of something.

Jonathan let the quiet stretch that extra heartbeat too long—just long enough for the weight of it to settle—before shifting his focus to Malik.

"Alright," he said. "That's the kids. Now tell them about Carter."

A tension like a drawn bowstring pulled through the room.

Malik sighed, thumb rubbing along the edge of his phone. "Okay," he said. "Here's where we are. As you all know, we couldn't wire her the traditional way. Full body wire, standard RF transmitters—too risky. These guys sweep for that. So, we embedded a micro cam and mic in the pendant of the replica necklace. Low power, low signature. Enough for intermittent video and audio."

He tapped the tablet and turned it so that the table could see the screen. A still image filled the display: a grainy wash of light through coarse fabric.

"This is the last usable frame we got before things went dark," Malik said. "By this point, she'd already been grabbed. Bag over her head. We had intermittent feed—rough, but workable—for about eight to ten minutes after that. Then…"

He swiped to a signal graph. A jagged line dipped and dipped until it flatlined.

"Then we started losing her," he said quietly. "Video dropped first. Audio went to static. Then nothing. Hard cut."

Kristian frowned. "They found the cam and smashed it?"

Malik shook his head. "If they'd destroyed the device, we'd see a different pattern. Sudden drop, maybe some voltage spike. This looks like the signal hit a wall. It taper-fails, then dies. That's jamming, or heavy shielding. My guess? Some combination of both. They might have a jammer in place where they keep the girls, or the building itself is a deadzone. Thick concrete, reinforced steel, no windows."

"Can we localize it?" Eternity asked.

"Partially," Malik said. He pulled up a map overlay—streets and blocks, faint cell tower icons. "We were using nearby towers and timing offsets to triangulate while her signal was still bouncing. It's not GPS-level precise, but we can confine her last known area to this."

He circled a rough three-block radius in red.

Jonathan leaned over the table. "Industrial corridor," he said. "Back edge of East Valley."

Warehouse boxes dotted the screen—gray rectangles crowded together, alleyways and lots between them.

"Extra Space Storage is right there," Rita said, pointing to a green patch near the bottom of the circle. "East Valley location. There's also a junkyard, a couple of old distribution centers, and what looks like an auto salvage place."

Kristian stared at the map. "We've got Sonya's woods feeding toward this direction, a creepy sedan doing loops near Estelle's place, and now Celeste's signal dying here."

"Chaos isn't random," Sebastian murmured, echoing Celeste's earlier mantra. "Not when it keeps landing in the same neighborhood."

"Storage units make sense," Rita said. She sat forward, eyes sharp now. "You can rent one with minimal ID, pay in cash or with prepaid cards, come and go at all hours. No one questions noise at midnight if they assume it's someone moving boxes."

"And they don't even need just one unit," Maria added quietly. "They could spread things out. Girls in one unit.

Supplies in another. Transport gear in a third. Different locations across the city. Keep everything compartmentalized. If the cops find one piece, they don't get the whole picture."

Candace's hands were clasped so tightly on the table that her knuckles were white. "We should already be there," she said. "We're sitting here talking while she's... God knows where."

"We are not storming every warehouse and storage lot in a three-block radius without a plan," Jonathan snapped, sharper than intended. He closed his eyes for a second, reined himself in. "We do that, we spook them, they move the kids. They disappear. Kicking doors right now is exactly what they want us to do."

"And Carter?" Candace asked, her voice barely above a whisper. "What does she get while we 'plan'?"

Jonathan looked down at the tablet—at that last ghost of a frame from Celeste's camera. Just light, fabric, motion.

"She gets us using our heads," he said. "Not just our panic."

No one liked that answer. But they all understood it.

Silence stretched again, taut and fragile.

Then Sebastian straightened. "We'll go," he said, nodding toward Rita. "Rita and me. We take an unmarked, swing on the strip. Eyes only. No guns out, no badges flashed unless we have to. We start with Extra Space. They've got cameras on the gate, on the office. Gate logs. If a van came through there around the time the signal died, we might catch it."

Rita nodded immediately, already mentally shifting gears. "We can go in as a couple looking to rent a unit," she said. "Ask about pricing, unit sizes, climate control. It gives us an excuse to linger. To look around. See who else is using the place, and to see how the staff reacts."

Kristian opened his mouth as if he might object, then shut it again, teeth clicking. He rubbed at his forehead instead. "At least it's controlled," he muttered. "Better than rolling up with a SWAT team and praying."

Jonathan studied Rita and Sebastian for a long beat. "You keep it low-key," he said. "If you see anything that pings your radar—you do not engage. You do not try to be heroes. You call it in, you pull back, and you let us coordinate a response."

"Understood," Sebastian said.

Rita pushed her chair back, the legs scraping against the floor. Her heart hammered, not just with fear of what they might find—but with the desperate need to find something.

Across the table, Candace stared at Celeste's empty chair.

'You better still be out there,' she thought fiercely. *'Because if you die on us, I'm going to kill you.'*

"Thompson," Jonathan said, "keep scrubbing that last feed. I want every frame analyzed. If there's so much as half a letter from a billboard in the reflection, I want it."

"Already on it," Malik replied. He tapped at his phone. "I've got my team enhancing contrast and running pattern detection. If we see anything identifiable, you'll be the first to know."

Rita and Sebastian gathered their things—badges, keys, discreet vests under plain clothes. No raid gear. Just two people pretending to be small.

"Be careful," Candace said quietly as they headed for the door.

Sebastian managed a faint, crooked smile. "Now you sound like her," he said.

"Somebody has to while she's gone," Candace shot back.

Kristian stepped close enough to clap a hand on Sebastian's shoulder as he passed. "Don't be stupid," he said. "We already have one out there living on the edge."

Sebastian huffed a humorless chuckle. "Yeah, well. Someone's gotta be the first to walk into the lion's den."

Rita's eyes flicked to the board one more time—the three girls, their small faces smiling in frozen innocence. Then to Celeste's empty chair at the end of the table.

'Just hold on,' she thought. 'You'd better have us taking your picture down soon.'

***

The drive out to East Valley felt longer than the GPS specified.

The city blurred past the windows—blocks of apartments, corner markets, gas stations, all thinning gradually into sparser lots and low industrial buildings as they moved into the outer strips—the city's glamour didn't bother to come this far.

Rita sat in the passenger seat of the unmarked sedan, fingers drumming restlessly on her thigh. The glow from the dashboard washed Sebastian's face in pale green.

"You good?" she asked, eyes on the road but attention split.

He snorted softly. "Define 'good,'" he said.

"Not actively shaking. Not hyperventilating. Not trying to drive us into a pole."

"Then yeah," Sebastian said. "I'm in fantastic shape."

They passed a row of shuttered autoshops; metal roll-up doors tagged in overlapping graffiti. A semi sat idling beside a loading dock, headlights off, engine rumbling like a low growl in the dark. Above them, the sky was hazy, light pollution turning the night a dull orange-gray.

"Think she's here?" Rita asked quietly.

Sebastian's hand tightened on the steering wheel. "I think if I were running a trafficking operation and wanted to stash victims somewhere nobody questions comings and goings," he said, "this stretch is top of my list. Storage units. Old warehouses. Places you can rent by the month and disappear behind a lock."

The Extra Space Storage sign appeared a moment later—a glowing green-and-white rectangle near the road, the digital display beneath it cycling through "1st Month Free!" and "Ask About Climate Control!" in bright, friendly text.

Beyond the sign, the facility stretched in neat, sterile rows: green metal doors, beige walls, black iron fencing. A small office sat near the entrance like a guard post dressed up as a customer service center.

Sebastian flipped on the turn signal and eased into the entrance lane.

Rita's chest tightened as she took in the perfectly ordinary scene. The trimmed shrubs. The clean parking spaces. A couple of overhead lights hummed quietly.

So normal. So boring. So perfect for hiding something monstrous.

They rolled closer to the gate, and that's when Rita saw it.

"Look up," she murmured.

Sebastian followed her gaze. Mounted on the roof of the small office building was a massive satellite dish—far bigger than anything a basic storage facility should need. It was angled slightly off toward the industrial strip, cables running from its base into a metal conduit that disappeared into the wall.

"That's overkill," Sebastian muttered. "You don't need a dish like that to track late payments."

Rita felt the hairs on her arms lift. "Could be internet. Could be something else," she said. "If someone wanted to blanket this place with interference—"

"—they'd do it from there," Sebastian finished.

He took a quick photo of the dish with his phone before pressing the call button on the gate keypad.

"Extra Space Storage, East Valley. How can I help you?" crackled the voice from the speaker.

"Yeah, hi," Sebastian said, brightening his tone into a friendly-customer mode. "My wife and I just moved into the area. Looking for a unit. Thought we'd swing by, see what you've got."

There was a brief silence, punctuated by the faint sound of keyboard taps in the background.

"Oh, sure," the voice replied, more enthusiastic now. "Come on in. Office is open till nine."

The gate began to slide open with a metallic groan.

As they rolled through, Sebastian dropped his voice. "Thompson, you getting all this?" he asked, touching the small earpiece in his right ear. They weren't broadcasting anything heavy; they were just using it as a relay channel to Tech.

Malik's voice came through, faint but clear. "Yeah. Signal's clean out there. Whatever they're running on that dish is localized. Once you're inside the office, I might be able to piggyback on their network if you get me close enough."

"Copy," Sebastian said. "We'll get you a front-row seat."

He parked in one of the visitor spots and killed the engine. The neat rows of green doors stretched out behind the office like a maze.

"Friendly couple," Rita muttered under her breath. "Shopping for a place to keep our Halloween decorations."

Sebastian cracked a tight smile. "Or our terrible life choices."

They stepped out and walked toward the office. The interior was exactly as expected: neutral beige walls, a counter with a plexiglass divider, a display of cardboard boxes and packing tape stacked in neat pyramids. The air smelled faintly of toner and stale coffee.

A man in his late thirties stood behind the counter, wearing a polo shirt with the company logo stitched over his chest. His name tag read 'Trevor'.

"Evening," he said, offering a practiced smile. "How can I help you folks?"

Sebastian leaned casually on the counter. "Hey, Trevor. We're looking for some extra space." He winced theatrically, and Rita jokingly groaned. "Sorry. I know you probably hear that ten times a day."

Trevor chuckled. "More like twenty. You moving, downsizing, or just tired of tripping over stuff?"

"Little bit of everything," Rita chimed in, playing along. "We've got boxes, some furniture, couple of bikes. Some old electronics my husband swears he's going to fix one day."

"Those are collector's items," Sebastian added.

Rita rolled her eyes. Trevor laughed again, warming up to them.

"Alright, well, we've got a few sizes available," he said, turning to the computer. "You two local?"

"Yeah," Sebastian said. "East side. We drove past earlier and figured we'd check it out. Place looks secure."

Trevor brightened at the compliment. "We take security seriously," he said. "Gate code, individual locks. We've got cameras on all the aisles and entries. Motion-triggered. Management loves their gear."

He jerked his thumb toward the back wall, where a flat-screen monitor cycled through multicolored grids of security footage—small squares showing driveways, hallways, corners of the property.

Rita's pulse ticked up.

"Speaking of," she said, nodding toward the monitor, "that's a lot of cameras," — a verbal cue for Malik.

"Got you. If you see the router, get me a clear path to it with your business phone, Ortega," Malik uttered.

Sebastian casually set his phone on the counter in front of him, screen down, angled toward the small router blinking beneath the monitor shelf.

Trevor shrugged, half-proud. "Corporate standard. Helps keep everybody honest. We log all gate activity, too. People like knowing we're watching."

"Thompson, you in?" he murmured under his breath, lips barely moving.

On the other end, Malik's fingers were already flying over a keyboard. "I've got a ping off their access point," he replied. "Signal's decent. Give me...thirty seconds. Pretend you care about climate control."

"So," Sebastian said, louder now, directing his attention back to Trevor, "tell me about your climate-controlled units. I've got some electronics I don't want cooking in the summer heat."

"Good call," Trevor said, launching into his spiel. "We've got indoor units down this hall—temperatures stay stable all year. Costs a bit more, but—"

"Thompson?" Rita murmured under her breath as she pretended to study a brochure.

"Almost there," Malik said in her ear. "They're using a basic vendor system for the cams. Default settings. No one told corporate IT that not changing the settings was a bad idea."

On the monitor behind Trevor, the camera feeds flickered once, then steadied.

"Got it," Malik said. "I'm in. I've got remote access to their DVR."

Trevor clicked through unit sizes and pricing. Rita asked a few more questions, letting her voice rise and fall like a genuinely indecisive customer.

"We can go look at a unit if you want," Trevor offered. "Sometimes it's easier to picture what you can fit."

"Maybe in a few," Rita said smoothly. "Do you have many people coming in late at night? We work weird hours, so we'd probably be moving stuff after dark."

"Sometimes," Trevor said. "People come and go. Long as they've got a code, they're good. Why?"

"Just wondering about safety," Rita replied, letting her gaze drift—purely by 'accident'—back to the surveillance monitor. "You ever have problems out here?"

Trevor glanced at the screen too. Rita was hoping the screen wouldn't glitch as he watched.

"Couple break-in attempts over the years," he admitted. "Some vandalism. You get the occasional sketchy tenant. But mostly? Boring."

Behind Rita's ear, Malik's voice sharpened. "I'm scrubbing the last twelve hours of footage," he said. "Gate cams first. When did we lose Celeste's signal?"

"Twenty after seven," Sebastian answered softly, keeping his eyes on Trevor. "Roughly."

"Rolling back now," Malik replied. "I'll flag anything that pops."

Rita picked up a pen and doodled aimlessly on the edge of a brochure, heart pounding.

"Okay," Malik said. "Everything looks normal until about 7:30 p.m. That's when—hold up."

The footage on the monitor behind Trevor stuttered for a split second as Malik forced it into rewind, then dropped it back to 7:29. On the mirrored feed at headquarters, he slowed the playback and patched a split-screen view to the tablet propped beside his keyboard.

"Ortega, you're about to get a ping on your phone," Malik said. "Don't react. Just act as though you got a text. I'm pushing you a live clip."

Sebastian's phone buzzed on the counter. He slid his hand over it smoothly, flipped it, and unlocked the screen with his thumb.

"Babe, look at this," Sebastian spoke to Rita. She moved closer to view the phone. "Give us one second," he spoke to Trevor.

"Oh, no problem," he remarked as he stepped away from the desk.

A video feed filled the display—grainy night vision of the facility's front lot.

Then, on the tiny screen, two black Dodge Chargers rolled into frame, one after the other, sliding through the gate like sharks through water. Both were low to the ground, windows darkened to near-black, their movements smooth and deliberate.

"We got something," Sebastian murmured, his voice dropping instinctively.

Malik was already watching, patched into the feed in real time.
"Confirmed," he said. "I'm pulling timestamps now."

Neither Charger had tags. No front plates. No rear temps. Just clean, matte-black voids where identification should've been.

The vehicles idled side by side.

No one got out.

A moment later, a rusted gray van crept into view, headlights killing themselves before the gate fully closed. Its body was scarred with half-scrubbed graffiti, paint flaking like dead skin. The bumper hung low, eaten through by rust. No license plate.

Rita felt a chill work its way up her spine. "That's them."

The driver of the first Charger stepped out, hood up, hands buried in his jacket pockets. He crossed the pavement with practiced ease, approaching the van. Malik sharpened the image, but the man's face stayed swallowed by shadow—the camera angle wrong, the lighting uncooperative.

"Switching angles," Malik said.

The feed jumped to a rear-facing camera.

The Charger driver grabbed the van's back door and hauled it open.

Rita sucked in a breath she didn't realize she'd been holding.

One by one, women were pulled from the van.

Blindfolded.
Headphones clamped over their ears.
Hands bound.

They stumbled when their feet hit the pavement, disoriented, terrified.

"Jesus," Sebastian whispered.

Then another figure appeared—smaller, more controlled despite the fear in her posture.

Celeste.

Even in the grainy footage, they recognized her instantly. The braid that was meant to make her look younger. The way she regulated her breathing. The way she performed fear without letting it consume her.

"Positive ID," Malik said quietly. "That's her."

The driver shoved the women toward the Charger, opening the rear door and forcing them inside.

"Count," Malik instructed.

"One… two… three… four," Rita spoke quietly. Her voice broke. "Four victims."

"More were in the van," Sebastian replied. "They split them."

The Charger driver returned to the van and passed a thick brown paper bag through the window.

"Payment," Rita murmured.

As the van pulled away, a camera caught the driver's face for half a second—just long enough.

"Freeze it," Sebastian said.

"Already did," Malik replied. "I can clean that up."

The image stopped: scar near the mouth, heavy stubble, dead-forward eyes.

The Chargers peeled off in opposite directions.

Then the lot returned to stillness.

"They used this place as a handoff," Rita said. "A neutral zone."

"And that dish on the roof," Sebastian added. "That's not decorative."

Malik's voice cut in, sharper now.
"That dish explains why Carter went dark. It's a localized jammer. High-powered."

Rita and Sebastian exchanged a look.

"Then we're not done here," Rita whispered.

Sebastian locked his phone, slipping it back into his pocket, as though nothing had happened.

He smiled politely at Trevor. Trevor was rearranging the display at the front of the store.

"So," he said lightly, as if they'd been discussing nothing more than box sizes, "about that climate control."

4

Celeste studied her reflection, hardly recognizing the girl staring back at her. Her hair, once limp from stress and the stale air in the compound, now framed her face in soft, controlled waves, pulled into a style that somehow made her look even younger—more vulnerable—but also cared for. Human. Angela had done that with nothing more than a cheap comb, a drop of hair oil, and a handful of worn elastic ties.

Celeste lifted a hand to touch one of the perfectly coiled pieces, marveling.

"Girl, this is amazing," she breathed, unable to hide her admiration.

Angela's shoulders relaxed for the first time since they'd met. She brushed a stray curl away from Celeste's forehead, then stepped back shyly. "Thank you," she murmured. "Sorry I couldn't clip your edges, though." She winced as she said it, almost embarrassed.

Celeste huffed out a laugh. "I get it. These *pendejos* aren't going to give us any scissors." Her laugh softened into something darker. "I think they know what we would do with them."

(Dumbasses.)

Angela snickered—quiet but real—like laughter she hadn't allowed herself in weeks. The sound was small, fragile, but in this place, it felt like rebellion.

"If we get out of here," Angela started, her voice dropping to a whisper as if the walls might swallow her words. "I'll give you the real deal. A proper style. All the products. All the tools. I know how to make you look bomb."

Celeste's chest tightened—not with fear this time, but something like stubborn hope. Angela had said if, but Celeste wouldn't let that stand.

"We *will* get out of here," she said, each word steady, firm, like planting a flag. She turned away from the mirror and faced Angela fully. "I promise you that."

Angela blinked rapidly, trying to hold her composure. Living here meant swallowing dreams whole before they got you hurt. But Celeste's certainty cracked something open in her.

Before she could spiral into fear again, Celeste reached into the tiny fabric pocket sewn inside her jeans—one of the few things the kidnappers hadn't torn away from her. She pulled out a folded bill. Not much, but in this place, it might as well have been gold.

"Until then," Celeste said softly, pressing the fifty dollars into Angela's palm, curling the girl's fingers around it. "Let this be a reminder of your talent and that you are destined for greatness."

Angela froze. For a breath, she just stared at the money in disbelief—like she had forgotten what it felt like to be treated like someone whose work mattered.

Her lips trembled. Her eyes glossed with tears, she tried, unsuccessfully, to blink away. When she finally moved, she didn't speak—she simply stepped forward and wrapped her arms around Celeste, clinging to her with a mixture of gratitude and desperation.

Celeste hugged her back just as tightly.

In a place designed to break them, this small moment—this human connection—felt like a victory.

A reminder that they were still alive. Still themselves. And still fighting.

The scent of cheap cologne quickly entered the room; Celeste could sense that Enrique was approaching.
She provided a warning glance to Angela.
Hide the money. Stay calm. Don't draw attention.
Angela quickly put the money in her pocket and took a step closer to Celeste, as if proximity alone might shield her.

The other girls reacted differently.
They shrank.

Huddled on the floor or against the peeling walls, shoulders curled inward, eyes wide, breaths held. Their bodies spoke volumes—stories of fear, conditioning, and the constant calculation of danger. Even the smallest shift in Enrique's footsteps made them flinch.

Celeste felt her stomach knot with a slow, simmering rage.

The door groaned open.

Enrique stepped inside, filling the space with a predatory presence. His gaze slid across the room like a cold blade until it landed on one of the youngest girls—tiny, maybe eight or nine, curled into herself like she wished she could disappear into the concrete.

His lips curved. A slow, revolting smirk.

Celeste's heartbeat spiked.
'Not her. Not tonight. Not ever if I can help it.'

Before his attention was fully locked onto the child, Celeste straightened and moved a deliberate half-step forward.

"*¿Vas a seguir oliendo así cada día?*" she teased lightly, forcing a breathy, nervous laugh. "*Ese perfume está fuerte, Enrique. Nos vas a marear a todas.*"
(Are you going to keep smelling like this everyday? That cologne is strong, Enrique. You're going to make all of us dizzy.)

Her voice quivered just enough to sound believable. Vulnerable. Distracting.

Enrique paused, the smirk pulling toward her instead. "*¿Ah, sí? ¿Demasiado para ti,* Destiny?"
(Oh yeah? Is it too much for you, Destiny?)

Celeste lowered her gaze like a shy girl trying to hide a smile. "*Tal vez… pero prefiero eso a oler este cuarto todo el día.*"
(Maybe, but I'd rather smell that than smell this room all day.)

Angela tensed beside her, but Celeste kept her tone airy, casual—bait.

Enrique's chest lifted with a pleased, self-important chuckle. The danger in the air thickened, but at least now it was aimed at her.

"Well," he drawled, stepping closer, "*siempre puedo llevarte afuera por un rato. A que respires algo… diferente.*"
(I can always take you outside for a while and let you breathe something… different.)

The girls behind Celeste stiffened, terror rippling through them like a silent scream. Being singled out meant risk—pain—violation. They watched with dread so heavy it settled into the floor.

Celeste forced herself to swallow. To appear unsure. Young.

"*¿Ahorita?*" she asked softly.
(Now?)

Enrique nodded, eyes lingering on her in a way that made Celeste's skin crawl.

"*Sí. Tú. Ven conmigo.*"
(Yes. You. Come with me.)

He reached for her wrist—not violently, but with ownership, with entitlement—and Celeste let him. She cast one last, meaningful look toward Angela.

Angela's eyes glistened with fear. For Celeste. For herself. For all of them.

But Celeste gave her a tiny nod.

'I've got you. I'm not leaving you behind.'

Angela nodded back, barely perceptible, her hands shaking as she tucked her hair behind her ear.

Enrique tugged Celeste toward the door, guiding her out of the room with a pressure that threatened bruises. The heavy metal door clanged shut behind them, sealing the girls inside once more.

As they stepped into the dim hallway, Celeste inhaled slowly, steadying herself.

She'd gotten the wolf's attention. Now she had to survive it.

Enrique's grip tightened as he led Celeste down the dim hallway. The air felt heavier out here—thick with mildew, dust, and the faint metallic bite of old pipes. Water dripped steadily somewhere behind the walls, each echoing drop sounding like a countdown she couldn't see.

The corridor stretched on, lit by a series of bare bulbs—some dim, some flickering, some burnt out entirely. Their shadows jumped across the stained concrete floor, morphing and shrinking with each uneven pulse of light.

Celeste kept her head slightly bowed, counting steps, memorizing turns, mapping everything in the dark corners of her mind.

Left past a door with peeling paint.
Right at the intersection where the floor dipped.
Long stretch. Flickering bulb.
One more door at the end.

Enrique stopped there.

He unlocked it with a key she hadn't seen before.

The door creaked open, exhaling a stale breath of air that carried grime, sweat, and something sour—like old fear soaked into the walls.

"*Pasa*," Enrique said, pushing her forward.
(Go in.)

Celeste stepped inside. The room was worse than she expected.

A single lightbulb hung naked from the ceiling, its glow weak and unsteady, flickering every few seconds like it was struggling to stay alive. The strobing cast the walls in alternating shadow and light, making the stains—dark, circular, splattered—writhe like they were moving.

In the far corner, a mattress sat on the floor. No sheets. No pillow. Just torn fabric over discolored foam, the edges chewed up as if something had clawed at them. The smell coming from it twisted Celeste's stomach.

A small metal bucket sat near the mattress. No lid. No dignity.

The walls whispered neglect—patched cracks, peeling gray paint, a spiderweb of wires stapled loosely to the corners. A single boarded-up window sat on the right wall, the wood bowed inward, as if someone on the other side had kicked it repeatedly.

Celeste forced herself not to react. Not to recoil. Not to let her fury show.

Enrique stepped inside behind her, closing the door. The sound of the latch sliding into place made her pulse throb in her ears.

He leaned against the wall and looked at her—not with lust, but with evaluation. Studying her. Measuring her fear.

"*¿Sabes porqué te traje aquí?*" he asked, voice low.
(You know why I brought you here?)

Celeste kept her shoulders rounded, her gaze somewhere near the floor. "*No… no sé.*"
(No, I don't know.)

He approached slowly, each step deliberate. The bulb flickered above them—on, off, on again—like even the light was afraid of him.

"You're new," he said, circling her as though she were prey. "*Y algunas veces… las nuevas necesitan entender cómo funcionan las cosas aquí.*"
(And sometimes, the newcomers need a lesson on how things go around here.)

Celeste inhaled quietly, letting just enough tremor slip into her breath. "*¿Cuales cosas?*"
(What things?)

His lips curved at her fear.

"*Reglas.*"
(Rules.)

He stopped in front of her, raising a hand as if to touch her face. She flinched—enough to seem frightened, not enough to seem defiant.

Enrique smiled, satisfied.

"*Vas a aprender rápido*, Destiny."
(You're going to learn quickly.)

His fingers brushed her chin, tilting her face upward toward the sickly light.

"And if you don't…"
He let the unfinished threat hang between them.
It filled the room like smoke.

Celeste forced her eyes to remain wide, innocent, terrified. It wasn't hard—not in this place.

Not with that mattress behind her. Not with the flickering light struggling to keep the darkness back. Not with the door locked and the echoes of other girls' suffering clinging to the walls.

Enrique lowered his hand and stepped back, watching her with unsettling intensity.

"We'll see how you behave today," he said finally. "*Tal vez seas una de las buenas.*"
(Maybe you'll be one of the good ones.)

He walked to the door, unlocking it—but paused before opening it.

He paused, glancing over his shoulder.

"And *no hables con las niñas sobre este cuarto. No les des ideas.*"

(Don't talk to the girls about this room. Don't want to give them any ideas.)

Celeste nodded quickly, swallowing hard like she was afraid to speak.

Enrique approved of her silence.

He opened the door just enough to slip out.

Then it slammed. The lock clicked.

Celeste stood still, breathing shallowly, her heart beating against the bracelet on her wrist.

She had survived whatever this was—for now.

But the room's darkness seemed to lean closer, whispering its own warning:

You might not survive it next time.

The moment the steel door slammed behind her, Celeste's knees buckled.

She didn't fall—she wouldn't let herself fall—but her hand shot out, bracing against the damp, peeling wall as the sound echoed through the small, suffocating room Enrique had shoved her into.

The bulb above her flickered once, then twice, before humming with a weak, sickly glow.

Celeste pressed the back of her hand to her mouth, swallowing a tremor. The air felt thick, hot, wrong. She could still feel the ghost of Enrique's touch on her chin—cold, possessive, evaluating. The look in his eyes replayed in her mind, each time darker, sharper, more predatory.

Her heartbeat thudded unevenly against her ribs.

'You're okay. You're okay. You're okay.'

She wasn't okay.

She took one step toward the mattress and froze.

She could smell him on her—that cheap cologne, that lingering humidity of danger. It clung to her clothes, her hair, burrowing into her skin like a parasite.

She wrapped her arms around herself, fingers digging into her sides as if she could hold herself together by force.

'He wanted one of those girls.' Her chest tightened. *'He would have taken her right there if you didn't step in.'*

Her breaths came faster. Shallow. Panicked.

All the training in the world hadn't prepared her for this—the slow violence, the psychological suffocation, the way power hummed behind every word these men spoke.

She had gone undercover before. But never like this. Never stripped of her badge, her weapon, her team, her identity. Never in a place where no one knew where she was. Where no one could find her.

A tremor rolled through her shoulders.

For the first time since stepping into this hell, Celeste felt the crushing weight of aloneness settle onto her spine.

She moved toward the corner and crouched down, resting her forehead against her knees. Her hands trembled violently. She squeezed her eyes shut, trying to ground herself.

'Think. Think, Celeste. Get control.'

But every thought she reached for slipped away, drowned out by the memory of Enrique's smirk... the way he had tasted her fear in the air.

And the worst part?

She had given it to him.
He saw it. He enjoyed it.

Hot frustration burned behind her eyelids.

A small, broken sound escaped her throat—halfway between a sob and a gasp. She clamped a hand over her mouth, shaking her head as if she could force the emotion back inside.

But she couldn't. Not this time.

Silent tears spilled down her cheeks—unbidden, unwanted.

She cried for Christine. For Angela. For all the girls in the surrounding rooms. And for herself—not from weakness, but from the horrific clarity of realizing what she had stepped into.

This is real. This is what they live every single day.

Her chest hitched painfully.

A single lightbulb hummed overhead, flickering every few seconds, as if counting down the minutes until Enrique or someone worse returned.

Celeste tried to quiet her breathing, but her body betrayed her—shudder after shudder racked her frame.

She hadn't felt fear like this in years. Fear that crawled beneath the skin and settled there, pulsing.
Fear that whispered cruelly, 'you might not make it out.'

She lifted her head and stared at the battered metal door.

No handle on her side. No lock she could pick. No window. Just a slab of metal that sealed her away from the world.

"I'm not done," she whispered hoarsely.

Her voice cracked. Her throat burned.

But saying it anchored something deep within her.

She wiped her face with the back of her hand, though her tears kept falling.

"They're counting on me," she whispered again.

The tremors in her hands slowed. Her heartbeat steadied—not calm but controlled.

Her fear didn't vanish, but she held it, shaped it, turned it into resolve.

She pushed herself up from the floor, standing unsteadily, breath still ragged.

She moved to the mattress and sat gingerly, muscles tight, ready to spring at any sound outside the door.

She wasn't okay. She didn't have to be. She just had to survive. And keep her mind intact long enough to take this place apart from the inside.

She exhaled shakily and whispered into the flickering light:

'I'm here, and I'm going to get justice for you, Christine. And Angela. And every girl they ever hurt.'

Her tears dried on her cheeks, leaving salt trails under the dying bulb.

The sound of footsteps echoed faintly in the hallway.

Celeste straightened, wiped her face again, and swallowed her fear. She didn't know who was coming next.
But she knew one thing:

They wouldn't break her. Not here. Not ever.

The footsteps grew louder.

Slow. Heavy. Deliberate.

Celeste's pulse kicked into a sprint. She wiped her face quickly, forcing her breathing to steady even though her lungs felt too small, too tight. The dim bulb flickered overhead—once, twice—as if warning her.

The steel lock clicked.

Once. Twice. The door groaned open.

Enrique filled the doorway, his silhouette tall and dark, the flickering light catching the angles of his face. That same cheap cologne drifted in before he even stepped inside—sharp, invasive, impossible to ignore.

Celeste fought every instinct to recoil.

He didn't enter right away. He stood there, leaning against the frame, arms folded, eyes scanning the room as if taking inventory of her vulnerability.

"You're quiet," he muttered, amusement curling around the edges of his voice. "No crying? No screaming?"

Celeste didn't respond.

Silence was the only weapon she had left.

Enrique pushed off the doorframe and stepped inside, letting it shut behind him with a heavy thud. The air seemed to shrink. Celeste forced herself not to back away as he approached.

"Girls like you," he murmured, tilting his head as if studying her. "They act tough, but break fast."

Celeste clenched her jaw.

He noticed—and smiled.

He moved closer, slow enough that she felt every inch of the space narrowing around her. When he stood directly in front of her, she could feel the heat from his body. The bulb above them flickered, casting brief, strangled shadows across his face.

He reached out—not touching her, just hovering a hand near her cheek.
Testing the air. Testing her fear.

Celeste's stomach dropped.

Instinct screamed to move. Training screamed to stay still.

Her breath trembled.

"There it is," Enrique whispered. "I knew it was in there somewhere."

She flinched—barely—but he caught it, savoring it.

"You hide it well," he continued, eyes narrowing with unsettling appreciation. *"La mayoría de las chicas entran llorando. Suplicando. Pero tú… tú eres diferente."*
(Most girls come in crying. Begging. But you… you're different.)

Celeste swallowed.

He leaned in just enough that she felt his breath skim her skin.

"Different," he repeated softly, "is interesting."

Her pulse hammered in her ears.

'Stay calm. Stay small. Stay alive.'

Enrique shifted, brushing a thumb under her chin—not touching her skin, but perilously close. Celeste held her breath.

"It's funny," he murmured. *"Las que se hacen los valientes… Son las que se rompen más que nadie."*

(The ones who pretend to be brave… they're usually the ones who break more than anyone.)

Celeste forced her gaze downward, playing the role she knew he wanted. Her throat constricted, but she willed her body not to shake.

He stepped behind her then—suddenly, without warning.

Celeste stiffened.

His presence loomed over her shoulder. She could feel him watching every rise and fall of her breath.

"Entraste aquí actuando como si fueras dura," he murmured. *"Pero ahora te veo."*
(You came in here acting tough. But I see you now."

Her fingers curled into her palms, nails biting into skin.

"You're scared," he whispered. "You smell scared."

Her chest tightened violently.

A tremor escaped her—small, involuntary.

Enrique chuckled low. He stepped even closer. The space between them vanished. Celeste felt the cold wall at her back—and him blocking her only exit.

Her mind jolted with panic.

'Not now. Don't lose control. Not here.'

She tried to breathe. Her lungs rebelled, drawing in short, frantic bursts.

Enrique noticed. Of course, he noticed.

"You think anyone is coming for you?" he asked quietly. "You think someone out there even knows where you are?"

Celeste's heart twisted painfully.

Her team. Her family. Her lifeline.

They were coming—but they were blind right now. Helpless. Signal jammed. Tracking lost. She had never felt so disconnected.

So alone.

Enrique leaned down until his lips nearly grazed her ear—not touching, but close enough to scorch.

"*Aquí nadie sabe de ti*," he said through his teeth, "*y nadie va venir.*"
(No one knows you're here. And no one is coming.)

A tear she didn't authorize slid down her cheek.

Enrique straightened slowly, eyes catching the tear in the dim, flickering light.

He smiled. "Good," he whispered. "Cry."

Celeste tried to wipe the tear, but her hand trembled so violently that it betrayed her.

Enrique stepped back at last, only a foot or two, still close enough to trap her against the wall.

"*Ponte cómoda*," he said softly. "*Vas a estar aquí por mucho tiempo.*"
(Get comfortable. You'll be here a long time.)

He paused at the door, glancing back with one final, chilling look.

"No eres la primera chica que pensó que podía salir de aquí. Y no serás la última en darse cuenta de que no."

(You're not the first girl who thought she could get out of here. And you won't be the last to realize she couldn't.)

Then he slipped out, the door slamming shut with a brutal finality that rattled the weak lightbulb overhead.

Celeste stood frozen.

For several seconds—or minutes, she couldn't tell—she couldn't breathe at all. Her body trembled violently, adrenaline flooding her veins. Her chest ached with the effort to hold herself together.

When her knees finally gave out, she slid down the wall, fingers digging into the floor, trying desperately to anchor herself to something real.

Her breath broke into shuddering sobs—silent, desperate, suffocating.

Her control cracked. Her training fractured.

The reality of the nightmare she'd willingly walked into swallowed her whole.

But after the sobs faded to tremors, she lifted her wrist. Her fingers found the small, braided bracelet—pink, blue, white—still tied securely around her skin.

Christine's mother's prayer. A lifeline.

Celeste pressed it to her forehead, eyes squeezing shut.

"I'm still here," she whispered.
"I'm still here."

Outside the door, Enrique's footsteps faded.

But the echo of his threats stayed with her, vibrating beneath her skin like a bruise that would never heal.

***

Celeste sat stiffly at the long metal table, surrounded by the other girls from her room. The sound of utensils clinking against thin plastic trays echoed in the dim cafeteria-like space, but the noise barely registered. Her mind was still in that flickering room… still under that single buzzing bulb… still boxed in by Enrique's shadow.

She kept her gaze downward—fingers interlaced tightly in her lap. The bruising weight of his words clung to her, pressing against her ribs like a vice.

Angela slid into the seat beside her without a word, gently threading her fingers through Celeste's. Her grip was warm, grounding—the only thing keeping Celeste tethered to the present.

Angela's silence was understanding in its purest form. She didn't have to ask what happened. Every girl in this place knew the look of someone who had been cornered, tested, and evaluated, as if they were nothing more than merchandise.

Angela squeezed her hand again, firmer this time, her thumb brushing the back of Celeste's knuckles.

Celeste swallowed, but the thick scent of Enrique's cologne still sat in the back of her throat. She couldn't escape it. It clung to her skin like oil. She rubbed her palms against her jeans, trying—futilely—to erase the memory.

The overhead light above her flickered once.

She wasn't in that small room anymore… but it didn't matter. The flash of that dim, suffocating bulb replayed behind her eyelids like a cruel reminder.

She inhaled shakily and closed her eyes.

"Please... let my team have found something. Let them be closing in."

Angela felt her shifting, her trembling, and rested her head lightly against Celeste's shoulder—a quiet, unspoken gesture of solidarity.

Across the table, the smaller girl Celeste had defended earlier peeked up timidly, her eyes wide but grateful.

"Thank you, Destiny," she whispered, voice barely louder than a breath.

Celeste blinked, pulling herself out of her haze. She forced a small smile, though it didn't reach her eyes.

"You don't have to thank me," she replied softly. "You shouldn't be out here fending for yourselves. None of you should. And as long as I'm around, you won't have to."

The girl nodded and looked down at her food again, as if afraid to draw too much attention.

Angela tightened her grip again. Another girl—maybe twelve, maybe thirteen—leaned forward slightly.

"Destiny... are you okay?" she asked, her voice trembling with concern.

Celeste hesitated.

Every truthful instinct in her wanted to say no.
To say she was unraveling. To say Enrique had gotten inside her head, scraping at old places she thought were untouchable.

But she nodded.

"I'm okay," she lied softly.

But the truth was coiled deep in her gut: she was shaken. Violated in a way that didn't require touching. She had willingly walked into this place for these girls—but knowing the purpose didn't make the fear any less real.

She drew in a slow breath, grounding herself.

Then she turned to Angela, voice low.

"*¿Qué tan seguido pasa eso?*"
(How often does that happen?)

Angela's eyes darkened with something heavy—exhaustion, sorrow, the kind of resignation that came from living the same nightmare repeatedly.

"Whenever they want," Angela whispered. "Often times, it's a mind-thing. But… they don't get sexual *too* often. They want to 'maintain our purity.'" Her lip curled with disgust. "If anything happens to us… it lowers the money they can get."

Celeste's stomach clenched.

"*¿En serio?*" she asked, though she already knew the answer.
(Are you serious?)

The implication punched her in the chest—not just what had been done, but what could have been done. What still might happen if she played this role too well… or not well enough.

Angela nodded slowly, her eyes glistening. "*Para ellos somos mercancía. Nada más.*"
(We're merchandise to them. Nothing more.)

Celeste stared at the table, breathing through the tightness in her throat.

She was determined.

She would not let Enrique—or anyone else—break her. She wouldn't let these girls stay buried under someone else's control.

She looked around the room—meticulously—at the huddled groups of children, some barely older than kindergarteners, clinging to each other like lifelines. Their faces were empty, their eyes dimmed with the weight of things no child should ever have to carry.

Seven-year-olds. Ten-year-olds. Fourteen-year-olds. Girls who should've been in school, at birthday parties, on playgrounds.

Instead, they were here—branded as product, stripped of childhood and choice.

Her jaw tightened.

'*All of these girls aren't runaways,*' Celeste thought fiercely. '*They're stolen. Or worse.*'

She exhaled, long and steady.

She couldn't save them at this moment. But she could stay strong enough to be the spark that burned this operation to the ground.

Angela leaned her forehead gently against Celeste's.

"You did good," Angela murmured. "He didn't take you. That's something."

Celeste nodded—not because she believed it, but because the girl beside her needed to.

But inside?

Inside, she whispered a silent promise:

'*I will not let them hurt you. Not anymore. Not again.*'

And she clung to that vow like it was the only thing keeping her together—because right now, it was.

5

"Please tell me we've got something," Kristian said, though it came out more like a plea than a question. He stared at the whiteboard as if willing it to rearrange itself into an answer.

The board had become a chaotic shrine of desperation—photos, names, arrows, timestamps. Christine. Estelle. Sonya. Angela. The Friedmans. The Aguilars. The blurry shot of the van driver. The Chargers. The rusted graffiti van. The hidden women fumbling out of the back. And at the center, circled three times in red: Celeste.

Her face looked back at them with its confident, steady expression: a knife in all their chests.

Sebastian clicked his pen: the rapid clicking broke the brittle silence. "We ran facial rec on the driver of the van."

Candace picked up without missing a beat. "Roberto Ortiz. Forty-two. Affiliated with the West Coast Ryderz." She flipped through her notepad, though she already knew the information by heart. "He's got priors—possession, petty theft, intent. Low-level muscle. Not a mastermind."

Kristian's jaw flexed. "LKA?"

"Last known address is a place off Paradise," Candace replied. "Studio apartment, lives alone. No spouse, no long-term relationships. Neighbors say he works 'odd jobs,' which could mean anything from construction to delivery driver."

"Bring him in," Kristian snapped.

But no one moved. Not yet.

Rita cleared her throat carefully. "There's more you need to hear first."

Kristian turned, brows lifting. "What's up?"

Rita exchanged a look with Lucinda, then continued. "We dug deeper into the families. Cross-referenced finances, known associates, debts, and any contact with local gangs."

"Start with Estelle's family," Kristian said.

Lucinda took over. "Her mother and grandmother weren't lying about Estelle. But her extended family? They were in deep with the cartel about five years ago. Her uncle made a deal with the cartel boss to ensure his family was taken care of while the boss was in prison. Uncle didn't deliver, and the boss' family suffered a bit. The boss' crew made threats, but they died down when he disappeared."

"Disappeared?" Sebastian echoed.

"As in no trace," Lucinda confirmed. "And even though Estelle's mom wasn't involved, someone could still be collecting on old debts."

A long exhale passed around the room. A new motive—retaliation—opened like a fresh wound.

"The Hollands?" Kristian asked, voice gravel.

Rita nodded. "The Hollands. On the surface? Clean. But Nico…" She hesitated. "Nico has a gambling addiction. Bad. Sports bets, Vegas tables, underground rooms. His debt is in the tens of thousands—plural. He's borrowed from loan sharks, private lenders, and people he should never owe anything to."

Candace's hand went to her chest. "So Christine—"

"Could've been collateral," Rita finished. "Used as leverage. A warning. A payment. We don't know yet."

No one spoke for several seconds. The implications were too horrifying.

Lucinda stepped forward. "The Friedmans… they're clean. They weren't lying. They're genuinely good people with no criminal associations. No debts. No shady past. Sonya wasn't a target because of her parents' sins."

Kristian rubbed his forehead. "Which means Sonya was taken because she fit a pattern. Vulnerable. Afraid. Watched."

"And Christine—" Sebastian added. "Christine is seven. They violated their usual age range to take her."

"That's what concerns me most," Eternity whispered. She pointed to the board, to the photos of the younger girls. "This escalation means the operation is spiraling. Whoever is running this is either desperate or expanding. Neither option is good."

A heavy silence settled over the room.

Kristian finally broke it. "Where does this put us with finding Carter?"

Candace swallowed hard. "The satellite dish at Extra Space Storage suggests they're jamming signals. That means Carter's comms were likely blocked before she could send anything."

"And if they're blocking her signal," Malik spoke, "it means they know what they're doing. They're not amateurs. They're running something big—bigger than local trafficking. Big enough to require blackout procedures."

Kristian closed his eyes briefly. "She could be anywhere."

"Not anywhere," Malik corrected. "Their vehicles, the direction of travel, and Ortiz's involvement narrow it down. They're using storage units, warehouses, or abandoned rentals. Places that are easy enough to move people around."

"And we know they use the Extra Space facility as a hub," Rita added. "Which is how they moved her."

Kristian slammed his notebook shut. "That's it. Ortiz leads us to the hub. The hub leads us to Carter. We're not wasting another second."

He started for the door, but Sebastian called out, "Hold up."

Kristian froze.

Sebastian stood, arms folded. His eyes were dark with worry. "Before we rush into this—Carter could already be in transit again. We've seen them do quick turnovers. And if she's being moved, Ortiz won't know where yet."

"So, what are you suggesting?" Kristian pressed.

"That we hit Ortiz hard and fast," Sebastian said. "Figure out what he knows based on their patterns. But none of us should be stagnant. While Rita and I go after him, the rest of you work the storage facility angle again. There's gotta be something there we haven't uncovered."

Rita nodded. "We already pulled the video, but now that Malik cracked part of their system, he might be able to get deeper—maybe even locate which units they accessed that night, if any. It could very well just be a hub where they make exchanges because of the jammer."

Kristian breathed slowly. He was a man on the verge— caught between command and raw fear for Celeste.

Finally, he nodded. "Alright. Ortega, Gaines—go. Bring Ortiz in."

Rita and Sebastian grabbed their gear, urgency vibrating off them like heat.

Candace stepped forward. "And us?"

"You," Kristian said, "are going to find where Carter was taken next. Because we are *not*—" His voice cracked, just slightly. "We are *not* losing her."

As the team scattered into motion, the whiteboard remained, dense with faces of the missing.

At the center, Celeste's eyes looked out.

Waiting. Depending on them.

And the clock was still ticking.

Rita and Sebastian moved quickly through the hall, their footsteps echoing sharply against the tile floor. This wasn't a normal operation. Not anymore. Not with Celeste missing. Not with the board full of children who depended on them.

By the time they reached the parking lot, Sebastian was already unlocking the SUV.

"You think Ortiz is gonna cooperate?" Rita asked as she slid into the passenger seat.

"He'll talk," Sebastian said, starting the engine. His eyes hardened in a way she'd only seen a few times before. "One way or another."

They pulled out of the lot and sped toward Paradise—sirens off, but urgency pulsing with every turn.

Kristian stood in front of the whiteboard again; hands braced on the edge as if the board were the only thing keeping him upright.

"Thompson, you got anything new on that storage facility?" he asked, voice stiff.

Malik's spoke as he worked on his laptop, "I'm inside their network again. Ortega's previous proximity earlier helped me establish a backdoor. I'm scrubbing their hidden directories."

"Hidden directories," Candace repeated. "Why would a storage facility need hidden directories?"

"Because," Malik replied as he typed, "they aren't a storage facility anymore."

A chill passed through the room.

Eternity leaned forward. "Meaning?"

"Meaning," Malik explained, "someone rewired their internal system. They built a shadow layer beneath the legitimate operation—unlisted cameras, unregistered unit timestamps, and encrypted visitor logs."

Kristian's head snapped up. "Encrypted?"

"Military-grade," Malik corrected. "Carter was taken somewhere carefully planned. They know how to make people disappear."

Candace swallowed. "So, you're saying this goes deeper than we figured?"

"I'm saying this is an organized pipeline," Malik said. "One clean enough to blend into everyday commerce. One dirty enough to traffic women and children across state—or national—lines."

Lucinda's pulse thrummed. "If they moved Celeste into that pipeline—"

"We'll get her out," Kristian growled. "We're not guessing. We're hunting."

***

Rita moved first, sweeping her flashlight across the barren apartment as a chill crept up her spine.

"Ortega…" she whispered.

The place was stripped almost completely—no furniture, no personal items, no clothes. Just a stained mattress in the corner and a small sofa. It didn't look lived in. It looked used. Temporary. Disposable.

A place someone stayed only long enough to do a job.

"Someone bailed fast," Sebastian said, eyes narrowing as he scanned the room. "They knew we were coming."

Rita stepped further inside, boots sticking slightly to the bleach-streaked floor. The chemical smell made her throat tighten.

Then she froze.

"Over here."

Pinned crookedly to the wall above the folding chair was a photograph.

A single, grainy image. Of Celeste.

Sebastian's posture snapped taut as he joined her.

It was a surveillance-type photo taken from a distance—Celeste walking under the streetlamp the night she went undercover, shoulders slouched, hair tied differently, clothing mismatched to make her look younger. Vulnerable. Alone.

Rita swallowed hard. "They were watching her."

"They tracked her movements," Sebastian murmured.

"But for how long?" Rita whispered. "And why her? There were dozens of girls on that strip…"

Sebastian shook his head. "Because she fit their profile. Small, young-looking, alone. They had no idea who she really was."

Rita exhaled shakily. "They still don't."

"Good," Sebastian replied. "If they did, they wouldn't keep her alive."

Rita's pulse hammered. "Then they took her because she was useful to them."

"That's what scares me," Sebastian said quietly as they exited the apartment.

Before either could say more, his phone buzzed sharply.

He answered. "Yeah?"

Malik's voice came through fast, tight, urgent, "tell me you two are close to the storage facility."

Sebastian frowned. "We're just leaving Ortiz's place."

"Head to Extra Space," Malik ordered. "Now. I found a buried camera network in their system. Not the public feed. A hidden layer."

Rita's eyes widened. "Hidden?"

"A shadow system," Malik said. "Encrypted angles, weird blind spots, activity that isn't logged in the main feed. And movement around the time Celeste vanished."

Sebastian's grip on the phone tightened. "We're headed there."

He hung up.

They left the apartment without looking back at the photo of Celeste fluttering slightly on the wall as the door closed behind them.

***

Kristian stood cramped beside Malik's workstation, tension radiating off him in waves.

"What are we looking at?" he demanded.

Malik didn't glance up. "Extra Space Storage wasn't just holding units. Someone installed unauthorized hardware—cameras, routers, motion sensors. All hidden under the legitimate system."

Candace stiffened. "So, the kidnappers, or someone in the organization, is well versed in tech and knows what they're doing."

"Exactly," Malik said. "And that satellite dish? It's a high-strength signal jammer that is activated at will. Anything within a quarter-mile loses transmission capability."

Kristian swore. "Carter's device never stood a chance."

"They knew the blind spot," Malik said. "But they didn't know she had backup."

Eternity hovered closer. "Anything on the girls who were taken with her?"

"Not yet," Malik said. "But the shadow feed from the night she disappeared? That's what I need Ortega and Gaines on-site for. Signal gets clearer when someone's physically in the vicinity."

Kristian's jaw clenched. "Good. They'll be there soon."

***

The SUV roared down Paradise Road, siren off but urgency thick enough to choke on.

Rita gripped the door handle. "Sebastian... the photo. They stalked her."

"They stalk all the girls," Sebastian said. "They didn't pick her because she's Celeste. They picked her because she looked like Destiny."

Rita stared out the window, voice shaking. "If they stalk all of them, that means planning. Structure. They're not just predators—they're organized."

"Exactly." Sebastian changed lanes sharply. "They'll slip if we push hard enough."

Rita forced a breath. "She's alive. She has to be."

"She's Celeste," Sebastian said. "She's survived worse."

But neither of them entirely believed the reassurance.

The storage facility loomed dark and quiet, its rows of metal units lined up like soldiers. The office lights glowed faintly at the front.

They stepped from the SUV. Gravel shifted beneath their boots. A cold wind snaked between the storage rows.

Sebastian lifted the tablet Malik had routed to him.

"Malik, we're here. You still linked?"

"Yep," Malik answered, keys clacking in the background. "Your proximity helps me piggyback their internal network. I'm pulling the hidden feed now."

Static fuzzed across the tablet screen.

Rita tensed.

Trevor stepped out of the office. "You all are back. You decide on the unit you want?"

"Save it," Rita immediately responded.

Sebastian flashed his badge and spoke quickly, deliberately vague.

"Police. We need access to your security room."

Trevor was visibly nervous with fidgeting hands. He blinked, startled. "I—uh—yeah, of course. Is something wrong?"

Sebastian didn't answer. "Open it."

The manager nodded quickly and led them inside.

The manager's security room was cramped—concrete walls, humming equipment, the faint smell of ozone and overheated plastic. The router blinked steadily in the corner, cables snaking outward like veins.

The moment they crossed the threshold, Malik made a triumphant noise over the radio.

"This puts us within range," Malik said. "Latency just dropped."

The feed refreshed. Clearer. Sharper.

Row after row of time-stamped footage came into focus—angles the facility didn't publicly advertise.

Rita drew closer, heart hammering.

"Ortega… let's find out where Carter is. Thompson, be sure to save this video footage."

"Do you all have a warrant for this?" Trevor mustered the courage to ask.

"Do you want us to arrest you for obstruction?" Sebastian questioned.

Trevor didn't respond.

"Don't interfere," he ordered.

The screen flickered once, twice, and then stabilized into a dim, grayscale view of the facility's rear entrance—a camera angle that no legitimate storage company should have had.

Rita leaned in. "What timeframe are we looking at?"

"I synced the feed to the night Carter disappeared," Malik replied.

"Okay," Rita said softly. "Run it again."

The footage began the same—empty lanes, moths circling a light.

Then something subtle. A flicker.

Sebastian froze the frame. "There."

Rita leaned in. "That's not signal loss."

"No," Malik confirmed. "That's manual interference. Someone cycled the jammer briefly."

They advanced frame by frame.

The Chargers entered—but this time, they weren't watching the vehicles.

They watched the spacing.

"Pause," Rita said.

Sebastian stopped the frame.

The Chargers weren't just parked.

They were angled—creating blind spots between camera zones.

"Son of a bitch," Sebastian breathed. "They mapped the cameras."

"And look at this," Malik added. "The second Charger doesn't just linger at the end."

They resumed playback.

The second Charger circled the building—not randomly.

"Pause again."

Sebastian froze it.

The vehicle stopped briefly beside a unit door.

Empty.

"Why stop there?" Rita asked.

Malik was already isolating the data.
"Because that unit sits directly between two access nodes. Dead space for cameras. Perfect place to stash or transfer something unseen."

Rita felt her pulse quicken. "A secondary drop."

"Or a contingency," Sebastian said.

They continued.

This time, Rita noticed something else.

"Back it up five seconds."

Sebastian did.

When the Charger driver handed over the brown bag, another exchange occurred—almost invisible. A nod toward the second Charger.

A signal.

"They weren't just splitting the girls," Rita said slowly. "They were signaling their next moves."

"And this," Malik added, pulling telemetry. "That second Charger synced briefly with the network. That means someone inside was monitoring the jammer status."

Rita's stomach sank.

"This wasn't just a handoff," she said. "It was command and control."

"Yes," Malik replied. "And now that we're this close to the router... I'm pulling residual MAC addresses."

Sebastian straightened. "Names?"

"Not yet," Malik said. "But paths. And paths lead somewhere."

Rita looked back at the screen—at the still frame of Celeste being forced into the Charger.

"They didn't just kidnap her," she said. "They tracked her."

"And now," Malik said, voice firm, "we track them."
She stared at the screen—the frame frozen on the moment Celeste was pushed into the Charger—and whispered:

"Hold on, Celeste...
Just hold on."

6

The drive back from Extra Space Storage felt heavier than the desert night pressing against the SUV windows.

Rita couldn't stop replaying the new surveillance footage Malik extracted. The black Chargers, the van, the signals.

Her stomach burned.

Beside her, Sebastian gripped the steering wheel tightly.

"We're running out of time," he muttered.

Rita didn't disagree. Instead, she pulled out her phone and dialed Kristian.

He answered on the first ring. "Tell me you've got something."

"Meet us at Ortiz's LKA," Rita said. Her voice trembled despite her best effort. "We found evidence at the storage facility. We're going to circle back to his LKA to see if we may have missed anything."

Kristian didn't hesitate. "On my way."

Sebastian shot her a glance. "Good. We'll need backup."

They turned into the faded turquoise apartment complex less than ten minutes later. It was quiet—eerily so. A dog barked somewhere in the distance. A couple argued behind a closed door on the ground floor. A streetlamp flickered sporadically, barely keeping the parking lot lit.

As they approached building B, Rita paused.

"Something's different."

Sebastian saw it too. A light—on.
The blinds in Roberto's unit—slightly shifted.
A shadow—movement behind the curtain.

Sebastian whispered, "Stay sharp."

The two made their way to the second floor and approached the apartment unit. The door to Unit 2B opened.

A man stepped out—thin, jittery, eyes darting. He wore a backpack slung over one shoulder and flinched when he saw them.

Rita inhaled sharply. "That's not Ortiz."

The man tried to slide past them to the apartment across the hall, but Sebastian blocked him with one outstretched arm.

"Las Vegas Police," Sebastian said, calm but authoritative. "Name?"

The man swallowed. "Javier."

Rita held up her badge. "You were in Ortiz's unit?"

Javier's throat bobbed. "I—I just needed to grab something."

"Funny," Sebastian said. "When we were here earlier, the place was empty. Completely cleared out."

Javier's eyes widened. "Look, I—I don't want trouble."

"Then open the door," Rita ordered.

Hands trembling, Javier unlocked 2B.

The moment the door swung open, Rita's breath stuttered.

The apartment—abandoned only hours earlier—now looked lived in.

A half-eaten burrito sat on the counter. A blanket thrown over the couch. A beer bottle sweating on the table. A phone charger plugged into the outlet.

Sebastian swept the front room, weapon drawn. Rita scanned the kitchen—and froze when she spotted a duffel bag half-tucked beneath the table.

She put on her gloves, dragged it out carefully, and unzipped it.
"How did we miss this?" she whispered.

Inside the bag were several burner phones. Wads of cash. A stack of SD cards. A folded map of rural Nevada with circles around multiple abandoned properties. A legal pad labeled in block letters:

UPCOMING SHIPMENTS.

And beneath it—a second list. Initials. Dates.

Rita's pulse spiked.

This wasn't just criminal activity. It was logistics.

Bootsteps thundered up the stairwell.

Kristian burst into the unit, breath tight, eyes sharp. "Gaines? Ortega?"

"Here," Rita answered.

Kristian took one look at the spread-out contents of the duffel bag and exhaled harshly. "Ortiz was involved deeper than we thought."

Sebastian lifted the map. "Drop-offs. Secluded properties. Easy places to hide people."

Kristian's gaze snapped to Javier. "Why were you here?"

Javier hesitated, voice cracking. "Roberto told me if he didn't come back today, to clear his stuff out."

"That's bullshit," Sebastian snapped. "We were just here, and this place was empty. Now you're sitting in here like you live here."

Javier wiped sweat from his brow. "I wiped the joint earlier for the most part and I circled back to see what I may have missed. Brought some food," he stammered.

Sebastian grabbed Javier by the collar and pinned him to the wall. Rita immediately responded to his movement.
"Javier, I swear to God if you don't tell us something—" the image of Celeste came to mind and he put his arm to Javier's neck.
"Hey, hey, hey," Rita interjected as she stood to the left of Sebastian. "We are no good to Carter by roughing this guy up."

"Carter?" Javier questioned aloud.

"Don't you say her name," Kristian warned— his lack of interference demonstrated that he condoned Sebastian's actions.

"You're looking at obstruction if you don't start talking," Sebastian warned.

Javier trembled at the threat. "He said he pissed off someone high up. Someone he called *El Pesado*— The Heavy Hitter. Said this guy handled 'the younger shipments.'"

Sebastian loosened his grip and instructed Javier to sit.

Kristian stiffened, something dark passing behind his eyes. "You're saying they have a separate handler for the youngest victims."

Javier nodded as he sat on the chair.

"That means Christine…" Rita whispered, the name coming out like a prayer and a curse at the same time.

Kristian turned back to the evidence and made a decision on the spot.

"I need my laptop," he said.

Rita looked up. "Now?"

"Now," Kristian answered, already moving. "If Thompson can dissect this in real time, we don't waste a minute."

He jogged down the stairs, hit the parking lot at a half-run, popped the trunk of his SUV, and yanked out his department-issued laptop—hardened, encrypted, the kind meant for fieldwork when a scene couldn't wait for a lab.

He was back inside within seconds, breath sharp, jaw set.

Kristian set the laptop on the counter, flipped it open, and logged in. "Malik, you up?"

Malik's voice crackled through their earpieces instantly. "I'm up. Tell me you've got media."

"SD cards and burners," Kristian said. "Multiple."

"Good," Malik replied. "I can mirror the SD cards once they're mounted. For the phones, I need identifiers—IMEI, MEID, serial numbers. Anything you can read off the devices."

Sebastian slipped on gloves and pulled the phones closer, lining them up like evidence on a morgue table.

"Seven burners," he said. "Cheap prepaid models."

"Photograph them," Rita instructed automatically, already in case-mode. "And read me the IMEIs."

Sebastian flipped the first phone over, thumb working the back panel. "IMEI's under the battery tray."

He snapped a photo, then dictated numbers. Rita typed fast, her fingers flying. One by one, Sebastian called them out—IMEI, serial, model—until she had a full list.

"Sending now," Rita said, and tapped the message through.

Malik spoke, "Got them."

Kristian watched the laptop screen as Malik worked from the other end. "What can you actually pull from an IMEI?"

"If any of these powered on recently," Malik said, "I can query carrier-side logs and tower associations. Prepaids still handshake. Even if they don't have service—if they try—they leave a footprint. Calls, texts, activation attempts, anything that pinged a tower."

Files began populating on Kristian's screen as Malik pushed results back—timestamps, partial tower IDs, a map tile loading slowly.

Sebastian leaned in. "You seeing anything?"

Malik's voice sharpened. "One device lit up earlier today. Thirty-two seconds. Not long—but long enough."

Rita's breath caught. "Where?"

"Rural tower," Malik said. "Agricultural service range. Middle of nowhere." He paused. "And it's close—very close—to one of your circled sites."

Sebastian's finger slid along the map until it landed on the location starred harder than the rest.

"The barn," he said quietly.

Kristian's jaw flexed. "That's our first hit."

Malik wasn't finished. "Also—contact overlap. One of these burners briefly paired with a number already flagged in a cartel logistics case. Ortiz wasn't freelancing."

Kristian looked like he wanted to punch the wall. "He was a courier."

"A cog," Malik confirmed. "But cogs still touch the machine."

Silence thickened the room. Then Malik's tone shifted—lower, heavier.

"Team, I've got something else."

Rita gripped the edge of the counter.

"...I found Celeste."

Sebastian went still, every muscle in his face tightening.

Kristian's voice dropped to something dangerous. "Where?"

"Video files on one of the SD cards," Malik said. "Holding location. Controlled environment. Multiple victims present." He exhaled shakily. "She's alive."

Rita blinked hard, swallowing the sting behind her eyes.

Kristian stared down at the starred barn on the map like it had personally insulted him.

"We move tonight," he said. "No delays."

Malik's voice stayed steady, but it carried a tremor of anger under the calm. "I'll keep cycling the IMEI queries. If any burner lights up again, I'll catch it immediately."

Kristian snapped the laptop shut with finality.

"Do it," he said. "And keep her on that screen as long as you can."

Because now they didn't just have evidence.

They had a pulse.

And they were finally close enough to chase it.
∎∎∎

Back at the compound, Celeste flinched as a sharp cry echoed from the hallway. She rushed to the doorway and saw one of the younger girls—Marisol—being yanked by the wrist by one of the guards.

"*¡No! Por favor, no!*" the girl cried.
(No, please don't!)

Celeste's heart tore. She moved instinctively—

But Angela grabbed her arm. "No," she whispered fiercely. "Enrique is watching."

Celeste froze.

Enrique stood at the end of the hall, arms crossed, smiling. A cold, poisonous smile.

Marisol sobbed as the guard dragged her toward a room Celeste hadn't yet seen.

Celeste's throat tightened. How many times had this happened? How many more times would it happen?

She wanted to fight. Wanted to sprint across the hall. Wanted to tear the guard's arm clean off.

But if she blew her cover—
If she died—
She'd save no one.

She forced herself to breathe, though her hands shook.

A soft voice whispered beside her. "Destiny...?"

Celeste turned.

A small girl—the youngest in the room—peeked up at her.
Christine.

Her hair was tangled. Her cheeks dirty. Her eyes—huge, terrified—locked onto Celeste's wrist.

Onto the bracelet.

Her bracelet.
The one her mother gave Sebastian, that he gave to Celeste.
The one Celeste swore she'd bring back.

Christine's breath hitched.

"That's... that's my mommy's...Mommy's bracelet..." she whispered—barely audible.

Celeste's throat tightened. She could not react. Could not break cover.

So, she did the only thing she could —
She pressed one finger to her lips, a tiny gesture shielded by her sleeve.

Christine blinked.
Clutched the crate beside her.
Nodded.

Then slipped away before anyone noticed.

Celeste felt tears burn her eyes.

'Christine is alive. She saw me. She knows someone is here for her.'

For the first time since being taken, hope cut through the darkness.

7

The black SUVs tore down the dirt road, headlights cutting through the desert darkness. Dust rose behind them in thick plumes. The old dairy farm loomed ahead—its silhouette jagged against the moonlit sky.

Kristian opened and slammed the door shut as soon as the SUV stopped. Rita and Sebastian were right behind him, weapons drawn, adrenaline scorching their veins.

"Move!" Kristian barked.

They split into formation, flashlights carving through the abandoned property. The barn door creaked open with a rusty groan. Rita's stomach twisted as she entered.

Nothing.

The barn was hollow. Empty. Cold.

Sebastian checked the loft—bags of feed long rotted, owl droppings, broken rafters.

Kristian kicked a metal bucket across the floor. It clanged and spun before falling still.

"Damn it!" he shouted, voice echoing through the cavernous space.

Rita rubbed her arms, shivering from more than the temperature. "We were so close. Malik said Celeste was here."

She could feel Kristian's fury radiating beside her.

Sebastian crouched near tire tracks. "Fresh. Hours old."

Kristian dragged a hand across his face. "We missed them by less than a day."

Sebastian exhaled slowly. "Carter was alive when that footage was recorded. We hold on to that."

Kristian didn't answer.

Rita whispered, "Let's regroup. Tomorrow, we hit every family again. We're missing something."

Kristian gave a stiff nod. "Fine. Bring them into the station. Get them out of their comfort zones. But tonight? We go home, we rest, and tomorrow—we tear this city up."

They walked back to the SUVs under a sky that felt too big—too indifferent.

And behind them, the empty barn stood silent, holding the echoes of children who were no longer there.

***

The conference room felt suffocating. Papers spread across the table. Photos. Files. The missing girls staring up at them.

Lucinda and Kristian briefed the others after speaking with Sonya's family.

"They're clean," Lucinda concluded. "They're devastated. Sonya had no involvement with anything criminal. If anything, they were overprotective."

Rita nodded grimly. "Then that's one family we clear."

Kristian flipped the Holland file to the top of the pile. "Next."

***

Nico and Leticia sat on opposite ends of the couch as though the space between them held all their marital cracks.

Leticia's face was pale. Nico's leg bounced uncontrollably.

Kristian studied them silently before speaking. "We're going to ask again—did either of you notice anything unusual these past few weeks?"

Leticia sniffled. "Just… Christine being scared. Asking about strangers. Nico told her not to worry."

Kristian turned to Nico, who refused to look up. "And you didn't think that was worth reporting?"

Nico swallowed. "I—We had so much going on."

"What kind of things?" Rita asked coldly.

Leticia's eyes flicked to her husband. "Nico…"

He finally looked up.

And Rita saw it—the guilt.

Nico swallowed hard. "I owed people money."

Kristian leaned forward. "How much?"

Nico shook his head. "Doesn't matter."

Rita's voice tightened. "It matters if you endangered your child."

Leticia let out a choking sob. "I knew something was wrong! He kept saying everything was fine. I didn't know—

"What did you do?" Sebastian demanded.

Nico broke.

He put his face in his hands and sobbed. "I didn't know they'd take her. I swear—I thought they just wanted leverage—just a guarantee until I paid—"

Rita's chair screeched backward as she stood.

"You sold your daughter for a gambling debt?"

Leticia wailed. "Nico, *¡Dios mío!*"
(My God!)

Kristian's voice cracked like a whip. "Who the fuck did you owe?" he didn't care about professionalism.

"I don't know his name!" Nico cried. "They call him *El Pesado.* He said they'd be monitoring Christine until I paid. I didn't know—I didn't know they meant—" He collapsed into sobs.

Sebastian's face was stone. "You gave them your daughter."

"Again," Nico spoke between sobs, "I didn't know that they would go this far with it! I've been threatened by them before, but now," Nico gazed into his hands. "God, where's our Christine. Bring her back to us," he spoke in a prayer.

Rita shook with rage. "You don't deserve to say her name."

Leticia, shattered, whispered, "Please… please find her…"

Kristian didn't answer.

He stood, jaw clenched, and motioned for the team to follow.

"Gaines and I are going to move on the location that Javier gave us yesterday for Ortiz. Hopefully, we can catch him before he tries to dart," Sebastian spoke as they left the room.

Kristian didn't utter a word.
Kristian's silence was deafening, and Sebastian could tell where his head was.

"Be on standby in case we need you," Rita remarked, cold and direct.

Kristian nodded his head.

Rita and Sebastian left without looking back.

***

Rita notified Kristian as she and Sebastian arrived outside Roberto's building.

"Hudson, meet us here. Now."

Minutes later, the three stood shoulder-to-shoulder, knocking on Roberto's door.

He opened it halfway—then paled when he saw them.

"Uh—Can I—?"

Kristian shoved the door inward and pinned Roberto against the wall. "Sit. Now."

Roberto stumbled into a chair. "I don't—I don't want trouble—"

"Too late," Sebastian said, tossing the duffel bag they'd found onto the table. "Recognize it?"

Roberto's eyes darted. "I—I just move things. I don't ask questions."

Kristian slammed his open hand on the table. "Those 'things' are children."

Roberto shook, sweating hard. "You don't know who you're messing with. These people—they don't leave witnesses. They don't leave loose ends."

Sebastian stepped closer, lowering his voice. "I don't leave loose ends," he threatened. "Celeste Carter is missing. That's *our* detective. *Our* partner. *Our* family. And y*ou* delivered her like a package."

Roberto blanched. "I swear, I didn't know she was a cop!"

"What fucking difference does it make? You knew she was a person," Sebastian responded.

Kristian stiffened.
Rita's stomach dropped.

Definite confirmation.

She's alive.
And they don't know who she really is.

It was the smallest blessing in a nightmare.

Sebastian's tone sharpened. "Where did you take the girls after Extra Space Storage?"

Roberto squeezed his eyes shut. "I handed them off. That's all I do. Pick up, drop off. I don't ask names."

Kristian yanked him forward by the collar. "Give me something, Roberto, or I swear—"

"THERE'S A FARM!" Roberto shouted.

Silence.

"An old dairy farm—off Route 9, past the dry creek. They use it for holding groups… sorting them… before transport."

"Transport where?" Sebastian pressed.

"To the border… or auctions… or safehouses—"

Kristian shoved him back, disgusted. "We already checked the farm. It was empty. Give us more."

Roberto trembled. "…Okay. Okay. There's another place. They move them again after the farm. A container yard. South industrial district. They load the girls into shipping containers. Sometimes for transport… sometimes for storage."

Rita felt her pulse throb in her ears.
"Storage? Are you fucking serious?" she asked.

Kristian looked at Sebastian. "Gear up. South industrial, we move tonight."

8

Celeste sat with the girls in the dim room, back pressed against the wall, heart still racing from the encounter the day before.

Angela sat beside her, pressing close like a sister. The younger girls huddled near them, drawing comfort from proximity.

Christine leaned into Celeste's side, trembling. "Destiny… are we gonna be okay?"

Celeste stroked her hair, forcing her voice steady. "Yes, sweetheart. I promise."

But Christine kept staring at Celeste's bracelet.

"That's my mommy's," she whispered. "You know my mommy?"

Celeste's throat tightened. She realized Christine's curiosity would cause her to continue to probe. "Yes. She's waiting for you."

From behind them, Angela inhaled sharply.

Celeste looked up.

Angela's eyes were wide—shocked—not scared but stunned.

"You're not one of us," Angela whispered. "You're... you're here to save us."

Celeste's breath caught. She grabbed Angela's hand. "You can't tell anyone. Please."

Angela nodded fiercely. "I won't. I swear."

But even as she promised, her gaze flicked toward the door—nervous.

Because she could hear footsteps—Enrique's footsteps.

The door opened slowly.

Enrique leaned against the frame, watching Celeste with a smirk that made her stomach twist.

Something in his expression had shifted.

Suspicion. Interest. Danger.

He stepped inside.

"Destiny," he drawled, *Necesitamos hablar."*
(We need to talk.)

Angela squeezed Celeste's hand, fear buzzing between them.

Celeste stood.

And tried not to show the tremor that ran through her.

The hallway was dim, lit by a single bare bulb that buzzed overhead. The concrete floor was cold beneath Celeste's bare feet, contrasting sharply with the heat crawling up her spine.

Enrique walked ahead of her, not bothering to look back—he knew she would follow. They always did.

Celeste kept her breathing steady, small, shallow breaths as though she were terrified beyond thinking. Her mind, however, worked at a sprint.

'Don't react. Don't slip. Don't give him anything.'

Enrique pushed open a door at the end of the hall. The room inside was small—concrete walls, a single chair, no windows. An interrogation room built for breaking spirits, not gathering information.

He pointed to the chair. "Sit."

Celeste obeyed, lowering herself slowly, carefully, trying not to reveal the tension in her muscles.

Enrique leaned against the wall, arms crossed. He was silent for almost a minute.

Watching her. Studying her.

"You're an odd one," he finally murmured.

Celeste blinked innocently. "I—I don't understand."

"Estás demasiado tranquila," he said. *"Demasiado,… observadora."*
(You're too calm. Too… observant.)

He crouched in front of her, face inches from hers.

"Girls come in here crying. Begging. You didn't."

Celeste widened her eyes just enough. "I was scared."

"*¿Ah, sí?*" his voice dropped lower. "*¿O estabas pensando en otra cosa…?*"
(Were you? Or were you thinking?)

Her stomach clenched.

He reached out and lifted her chin with two fingers. "*¿Y tú quién eres, Destiny?*"
(Who are you, *Destiny*?)

Destiny. The name she'd given them.

She forced a tremble into her voice. "Destiny Rojas. I told you."

He tilted his head, studying her like she was a puzzle with too many wrong pieces.

"You carry yourself well for a sixteen-year-old who 'ran away.' You pay attention. You protect others." His eyes narrowed. "And that little one—Christine. She looks at you like she knows you."

Celeste's pulse thudded so loud she feared he could hear it.

"I don't know. She just… she's scared."

Enrique smiled slowly.

"Kids that age don't cling to strangers unless they feel safe. And you? You make her feel safe." He leaned closer. "*Me hace preguntarme.*"
(Makes me wonder.)

Celeste kept her voice small. "I'm sorry."

"Don't apologize." He stood. "*Vamos, dime la verdad.*"

(Just tell me the truth.)

She swallowed. "I told you. I'm just… Destiny."

Enrique stared for a long, cold moment.

Then he opened the door.

"*Ven. Vamos a devolverte con las demás.*"
(Come. Let's get you back to the others.)

The two of them exited the 'interrogation' room and reentered the room with the girls.

The moment Celeste stepped inside, Christine bolted toward her and wrapped her tiny arms around Celeste's waist.

"Destiny!" she whispered urgently, face buried in Celeste's shirt.

Angela's eyes went wide—fear, recognition, concern.

Celeste knelt, smoothing Christine's hair. "Hey, it's okay. I'm okay."

Christine shook her head, clutching Celeste harder. "Don't go with him again. Please don't go."

Enrique's gaze cut across the room like a blade.

Every girl stiffened. Every girl knew what that look meant.

Angela moved instinctively, stepping between Enrique and Christine. "She's scared. That's all. The littles get attached—"

"Quiet," Enrique snapped.

Angela fell silent immediately, jaw tight.

Enrique looked down at Christine, then up at Celeste.

"You keep your distance from her," he ordered. "Both of you."

Christine whimpered and clung tighter. "No! Don't make me—don't make me leave Destiny!"

The outburst froze the room.

"It's okay," she whispered. "I'm not going anywhere."

But Christine cried harder.

Enrique's suspicion sharpened. "You two are getting a little too comfortable."

Angela stepped in, voice barely holding steady. "She's seven, Enrique. Seven. She clings to whoever and whatever makes her feel protected."

The word protected landed wrong.

Enrique's eyes slid back to Celeste.

"¿Eso es lo que estás haciendo?" he asked softly. *"¿Protegiéndola?"*
(Is that what you're doing? Protecting her?)

Celeste lowered her gaze, letting her shoulders hunch, shrinking herself. "I didn't mean to cause trouble."

Another long beat of silence.

Then Enrique stepped back.

"Dinner. Fifteen minutes."

He slammed the door behind him.

Only then did Celeste let herself exhale.

Angela crouched next to her. "He's onto you," she whispered. "He sees it."

"I know," Celeste whispered back. "But I'm not leaving her."

Angela squeezed her hand. "Then we protect her together."

***

Rita, Sebastian, Kristian, and the rest of the team stood gearing up near the exit of headquarters—vests strapped, weapons checked, vehicles ready.

The container yard was their next target.

Time was bleeding out.

Kristian grabbed the last file on the table. "Load up."

They reached the doorway—

And stopped.

The chief of police, Arturo Hale, stepped in front of them, arms crossed, expression thunderous.

"Going somewhere?" he asked.

Kristian stiffened. "Move, sir."

Arturo didn't.

"In my office. Now."

Rita muttered, "You've got to be kidding."

Kristian stormed past him into the office, followed by a tense Sebastian and Rita.

The door closed.

"What the hell do you think you're doing?" he questioned.

"Saving our deputy!" Kristian shot back. "And a dozen other girls!"

"You're acting without jurisdiction," Arturo snapped. "Without warrants. Without authorization. You have compromised evidence, illegally accessed surveillance, and obtained intel through methods that will get this entire case thrown—"

"To hell with a warrant!" Kristian slammed his fist on the desk. "Carter is out there with traffickers who move kids like cargo."

Arturo's jaw tightened. "And what happens when a judge reviews your methods? When a cartel lawyer gets involved? When this spirals into a federal cluster? You think they'll let you keep your badge after this?"

Kristian stepped closer. "I don't give a damn about my badge. If you want it," Kristian pulled it from his side, "take the shit."

Rita spoke up quietly but fiercely. "Sir… that's a seven-year-old girl. And Celeste. You're telling us to wait? For paperwork?"

Arturo's voice lowered. "I am telling you this mission is suicide. You don't know what's waiting for you out there. You don't have the manpower. You don't have the gear."

Sebastian clenched his jaw. "Then give us the manpower."

"You think I haven't tried?" Arturo barked. "We can't get a warrant for the yard. Their lawyers will bury us. We stand down until we have something solid."

Kristian stared at him with disbelief.

"Stand down?" he echoed. "While they move those girls again? While they—"

His voice broke.

Arturo softened only slightly. "I understand your loyalty, Kristian. But I'm ordering you—all of you—to stand down until further notice."

Rita shook her head. "Sir... if we wait—those kids are gone."

Arturo didn't answer.

That said everything.

The order was final.

The mission stopped cold.

And somewhere in the dark—

Celeste's time was running out.

The order echoed long after the office emptied.

Stand down.

Kristian barely remembered walking out of headquarters. Barely registered the weight of his vest being stripped off, the sound of lockers slamming, the silence that followed them like a curse.

Outside, the city carried on—cars passing, radios chirping, people breathing—while somewhere beyond the reach of paperwork and protocol, Celeste Carter was still undercover. Still exposed.

9

Dinner was always the worst part of the day.

The girls were herded into a long, low-ceilinged room, fluorescent bulbs humming overhead like angry insects. Metal trays clanged against the table. The meal—rice, beans, tough steak—steamed faintly.

Each girl moved carefully, quietly, like any sudden movement might provoke punishment.

Celeste took her seat at the end of the table.

Christine immediately climbed into the seat beside her, scooting close until their shoulders touched. Her tiny fingers hooked around Celeste's arm like it was the only anchor she had.

Angela sat across from them, her eyes flicking between Celeste and Enrique—who stood near the door, arms crossed, watching like a hawk choosing its prey.

Celeste felt his stare burning into her skin.

Christine tugged at her sleeve. "Destiny, can I have some of your rice?"

"*Claro*," Celeste murmured, sliding half her portion onto the little girl's tray. "*Come despacio*, okay? You don't want a stomachache."
(Of course. Eat slowly.)

Christine nodded, trusting her completely.

Maybe Christine was clinging tighter to Celeste because of her mothering nature.

Celeste kept her posture small, shoulders rounded—but her mind raced.

Enrique stepped closer.

"*¿Disfrutando la cena*, Destiny?" His tone was smooth but laced with something sharp.
(Enjoying your food, Destiny?)

Celeste didn't look up. "*Sí, señor.*"
(Yes, sir.)

"*Hablas bien*," he murmured. "*Y demasiado.*"
(You speak well. And too much.)

She swallowed. "*Solo quiero mantener la calma.*"
(Just trying to stay calm.)

"*¿Y proteger a la niña?*" His gaze cut toward Christine.
(And protect the girl?)

Celeste forced her breath steady. "*Solo… se siente sola.*"
(She just…. Feels lonely.)

Enrique smirked faintly—dangerously. "*Las niñas solas son útiles. Pero tú… tú pareces demasiado cómoda.*"

(Lonely girls can be useful. But you... you seem too comfortable.)

Christine stiffened, picking up the tension even if she didn't understand the words.

Celeste gently touched her back. "*Está bien, pequeñita.* Come."
(It's okay, little one.)

Enrique's eyes narrowed.

Angela offered a quick distraction. "Destiny's been helping all of us speak better and has been helping the younger ones learn Spanish or English... whichever they're struggling in. That's why she talks more."

Enrique didn't take his eyes off Celeste.

"*Después de la cena,*" he said quietly, "*quiero hablar contigo.*"
(After dinner, I want to talk to you.)

Celeste nodded.

But dread settled deep in her bones.

The moment the trays were collected, Enrique jerked his chin toward the hallway.

"*Camina,*" he ordered.
(Walk.)

Christine tried to follow, but Angela held her back gently. "*Déjala ir, mi amor.* Just for a moment."
(Let her go, my love.)

Christine whimpered but obeyed.

Celeste stepped into the hallway.

Enrique didn't take her to the interrogation room. He simply cornered her between two crates stacked against a concrete wall.

His tone dropped to something colder.

"*No juegues conmigo*, Destiny."
(Don't play with me, Destiny.)

"I'm not," Celeste answered, keeping her eyes down.

"You think I don't see the way the little one looks at you? *Como si fueras su salvadora*."
(As if you are her savior.)

Celeste's heart thudded. "*Sólo la calmé*."
(I just calmed her down.)

"No." He leaned in closer, breath brushing her cheek. "*Tú no eres cualquiera. No eres normal*." His voice sharpened. "*¿Quién eres realmente?*"
(You're not just *anybody*. You're not normal, Who are you really?)

Celeste forced her hands to shake. "*Yo… no sé qué quiere que diga*."
(I don't know what you want me to say.)

Enrique studied her—long and hard.

"*Voy a descubrirlo*," he whispered.
(I'm going to find out.)

He stepped back and walked away.

Celeste exhaled slowly, her stomach twisting so violently it hurt.

'*He's testing me. He's circling. I'm running out of time.*'

When she returned to the room, Christine launched into her arms, trembling.

"Don't leave again," she whispered.

Celeste knelt in front of her, bringing herself to the child's level. She held her tight, hiding her fear. "*No voy a ninguna parte.* Not tonight, not ever."
(I'm not going anywhere.)

Christine searched her face, as if testing the truth of it.

Angela moved closer, placing a hand over Christine's smaller one. "We'll protect you. Together."

■■

Kristian didn't hear that promise.

What he felt—minutes later—was worse.

A pressure in his chest.
A wrongness he couldn't shake.
The same instinct that had kicked in every time Celeste had walked into a situation she shouldn't have survived.

The room felt too quiet.
The clock—too loud.

They were waiting.

And Celeste didn't have time for waiting.

The window wasn't closing.

It was already closing on her.

Kristian turned back toward the Chief's office before anyone could stop him.

The door to Arturo's office slammed open once more, and Kristian stormed inside, face red, jaw clenched hard enough to crack enamel.

"You gotta be kidding me!" he shouted, voice shaking. "You're shutting us down? Now? When she's out there?"

Arturo closed a file calmly. "Lower your voice."

"Fuck that!" Kristian exploded. "Celeste is missing, and you continue to preach procedure."

Rita rushed in behind him, Sebastian right on her heels, both of them stopping short when they saw Kristian squared off at the desk.

"Kristian—" Rita started.
"No," he barked. "Don't tell me to breathe. Don't tell me to calm down."

He pointed at Arturo.

"He wants us to sit on our asses while Celeste is trapped with a trafficking ring that moves kids like livestock!"

Arturo's jaw tightened. "You have no warrant for that container yard. No probable cause that will hold in court. If you raid without authorization—"

"I don't have intel," Kristian cut in, voice low now— controlled in a way that chilled the room. "I have the same feeling I get every time Celeste Carter walks into something she shouldn't survive."

The room went quiet.

Arturo studied him for a long moment, then spoke softly. "So that's why you're back," he said. "This isn't about the yard or the girls. It's about her."

Kristian didn't hesitate.

"It's about all of them," he said. "She went under for those girls. She stayed when she could've walked. You don't get to separate her from them like that."

Arturo's nostrils flared. "Inspector—"

"We'll save her," Kristian said, stepping closer. "And we'll save every one of those girls."

Rita stepped between them, voice trembling but steady. "Sir. Please. We're running out of time."

Arturo shook his head, frustration bleeding into something darker. "The mission is suspended until further notice. You are not stepping foot near that yard."

Sebastian scoffed. "So, we wait for a body?"

"Don't twist my words," Arturo snapped.

Kristian gestured sharply toward the wall of evidence. "They're moving. You know it. Every minute we wait, we lose ground. The window isn't closing – it's slamming shut."

Arturo's gaze dropped to Kristian's chest. "You know what happens if you break protocol."

Kristian reached for his belt.

The badge came off with a sharp metallic click.

He didn't throw it.

He placed it carefully on the desk between them.

Arturo's gaze hardened. "You think laying your badge down changes anything? My stance isn't changing on this."

It doesn't," he said, voice low, almost a whisper—but with a weight that filled the room. "It's just proof I don't care what I lose. We'll save her. We'll save them all."

Rita grabbed his arm, whispering urgently. "Kristian—hey—no. We can't all get suspended. Carter needs us thinking clearly, not getting benched."

He shook her off, pacing like a panther trapped in a cage, letting his fire fill the space without speaking another word. His eyes stayed on Arturo.

Arturo stared at the badge for a long moment, then turned away.

"Stand down," he said, voice heavy. "That's an order."

Kristian's jaw tightened.

And when the door closed behind the chief, he didn't reach for the badge.

The team stood in silence.

The kind of silence that trembles. The kind that breaks things.

Rita looked at Kristian and noticed the fire in his eyes. She whispered to the team, "we're not done. We may be down but we're not out." She turned to Malik, who hovered anxiously at the computer station.

Her voice was low, urgent.

"Malik," she said, "I don't care how you do it. I don't care what walls you have to break or what systems you have to breach."

She leaned in closer.

"Establish contact with Celeste. I don't care if it's a ping, a static blip, a half-second signal. Just find her."

Malik swallowed. "You... want me to go rogue with it?"

Kristian didn't even hesitate. "Yes."

Rita nodded firmly. "Do whatever it takes."

Malik looked at all of them—shaking, terrified, but ready.

"I'll find her," he said.

Kristian turned back to the board, staring at Celeste's picture.

"We're not losing her," he murmured.
▪▪▪

The girls gathered in their assigned room as the dim hallway lights clicked off one by one, drowning the corridor in shadows. Celeste sat on her thin mattress, legs drawn in, watching the girls' nightly ritual—brushing hair with fingers instead of combs, laying out shared blankets, whispering prayers that were older than their trauma.

Christine curled up beside Celeste immediately, resting her small head against Celeste's arm.

Angela watched silently from her mattress, which was next to Celeste's.

"You okay?" Angela asked, voice hushed but pointed.

Celeste nodded, but her jaw twitched.

Angela moved closer. "Destiny... *lo que pasó con Enrique*—he never lets new girls go that easy."
(What's going on with Enrique?)
Her eyes narrowed. "Who are you?"

Celeste's pulse stuttered. Too direct.
"*Soy una chica más*, Destiny Rojas" she deflected.
(I'm just a girl.)

"No." Angela's voice sharpened. "*Tú no eres como nosotras. No lloras. No tiemblas.* You look at them like you're... studying them."
(You're not like us. You don't cry. You don't tremble.)

Celeste felt heat rise in her chest. Not fear—frustration. Suspicion cut both ways.

"Angela, I'm just trying to survive," she whispered.

Angela didn't blink. "You're hiding something. I can feel it."

Celeste's breath hitched. If Angela pushed too hard, she could blow everything. "I'm not your enemy," Celeste murmured.

Angela searched her face for a long moment, lips pressed tight.
A question, unspoken, lingered between them.

Before Celeste could respond, the door yanked open.

Enrique.

His silhouette filled the frame like a storm.

"Destiny," he barked. "*Ven conmigo.*"
(Come with me.)

Christine clung to Celeste's sleeve. "No—please—don't go," she whimpered.

Enrique's eyes flashed. "*¡Ahora!*"
(Now!)

Celeste peeled Christine's fingers from her arm gently. "*Vuelvo pronto, pequeñita.*"
(I'll be back soon, little one.)

But inside, dread churned like a tidal wave.

She stood.

Enrique grabbed her by the arm and dragged her down the hallway. His fingers dug into her skin, bruising already forming.

"*¿Qué hice?*" Celeste whispered.

(What did I do?)

He didn't answer.

He shoved her into a small, filthy bedroom—a single flickering bulb hanging overhead, a stained mattress on the floor, and nothing else.

"*Sueñas aquí esta noche*," he said coldly. "You stay where I can watch you."
(You're sleeping in here tonight.)

Celeste's stomach hollowed out.

He stepped forward. The door clicked shut behind him.

Her chest tightened. She swallowed air that felt razor-sharp. Her ears rang.

She knew what he intended. She had expected it.
But expectation didn't protect her.

As Enrique approached, Celeste's mind fragmented—part survival, part horror, part absolute refusal to break. Her breath hitched, hands trembling despite her will.

"*Querías jugar fuerte*," Enrique murmured darkly. "*ahora vamos aver que tan capaz eres.*"
(You wanted to play tough. Now we're going to see how capable you are.)

The bulb flickered overhead like a mocking heartbeat.

Celeste shut her eyes.

'*Team… please… hurry.*'

The emotional wound began long before anything touched her.
The violation wasn't physical—it was the stripping of control, the enforced helplessness, the way Enrique's breath filled the room and left no space for her own.

Hours later—she wasn't sure how long—the door finally opened. She was shoved back toward the hallway, legs unsteady, heart raw.

She returned to the girls' room quietly, without a word.

Christine rushed into her arms, sobbing without knowing why.

Angela's face knotted with fury and heartbreak.

Celeste sat there, holding the crying child, staring past the flickering light.

She had known the risks. She had prepared for the danger.
But nothing prepared her for the ache that burrowed under her skin and stayed there.

'Hold on', she told herself.
'If not for myself, I have to hold on for them.'

10

Malik hadn't slept.

His workstation looked like a warzone—empty energy drink cans, sticky notes, tangled cables, and a half-eaten protein bar he forgot about. His eyes were bloodshot, his hoodie wrinkled, and his fingers flew across the keyboard as if he were performing surgery.

He refused to stop.

Because somewhere out there, Celeste Carter was alone.

He rerouted frequencies. Tried new signal paths. Amplified and dampened interference. Nothing held.

Until—
A sudden spike.

A pixelated blip appeared on his monitor.
Then another.

Malik froze. "Wait—hold on—what is that…?"

He adjusted the gain. A tiny waveform trembled into existence.

Static hissed through his headset.

kkkkk—sssshhh—C... I... s... te—sshhhhh—

His breath caught.

"Celeste? Testing—Celeste, if you can hear me, change your position. Turn your head."

Kristian, who had been pacing behind him like a caged animal, stopped mid-step. "What? What do you have?"

Malik raised a hand, eyes glued to the signal. "Shh... I think she's—wait—"

The camera shifted slightly as Celeste turned her head.

"She can hear me," Malik whispered. A tear formed in his eye. "Celeste, we're coming. Just hold tight."

The monitor flickered violently.

Pixels formed shapes.
Shapes formed blurry color patches.
Then—

A flicker of movement.

A girl's shoulder.
Then the outline of a wall behind her.
Then darkness again.

Malik's voice cracked. "I'm getting a visual feed."

Rita rushed over. "From the pendant?"

"Yes—yes, yes—hold on—stabilizing now—" Malik typed faster. His hands trembled with adrenaline. "I can't get a full frame rate, but I can pull stills at intervals."

The video feed pulsed again. The first frame was a blurry silhouette – possibly a child. The second frame was of Celeste's wrist – the braided bracelet was visible.
The third frame went completely dark – the pendant was shifting under the clothing.

Kristian swore under his breath. "She's alive. She's fucking alive."

Rita covered her mouth as tears filled her eyes. "Thank God… thank God."

Sebastian leaned closer to the monitor. "Can you clean the audio?"

"I'm trying." Malik isolated frequencies, breaking them apart like puzzle pieces. A faint voice filtered through—muffled, distorted, but unmistakable.

"position…turn… head…."

Rita gasped. "That's you!"

Malik swallowed hard. "There's audio latency. The earrings are acting as receivers, and she can hear me. Let me try to clear the delay."

Kristian steadied himself against the desk. "What's her condition? Do we see injuries?"

"Not enough frames—yet." Malik dragged the timeline back. "But she's moving. And she's holding the camera close, intentionally or not. She knows she's transmitting."

Sebastian's jaw tightened. "Then she knows we're coming."

Kristian nodded sharply—determination in his eyes, but fear still flickering beneath the surface.

"Get me her coordinates," he ordered quietly. "Even if they're bouncing. Even if the jammer scrambles half of it. Get me something I can put boots on."

Malik wiped sweat from his brow. "Already working on it."

Rita whispered, voice trembling with hope and terror, "Celeste… just hang on. We're coming."

Malik leaned in, adjusting the gain again. "I've got a location ping—east of the container yard. Big structure. Possibly industrial. Could be a warehouse or a farm building."

Kristian grabbed his vest. "That's where we go."

Rita tightened her ponytail. "We're really doing this?"

Sebastian loaded his gear. "We're doing this."

Kristian swore under his breath. "Fuck Hale, fuck the delay, and fuck anyone who thinks we're leaving her there."

Rita placed a hand on his arm. "We'll get her."

Sebastian ensured his vest was secure. "You know if this goes South, we're all done for. Whether it be literally or professionally."

Kristian's jaw clenched. "Then it goes South with us saving them," he assured the team. "Thompson, Tell her… tell her we're coming."

Malik nodded once. "You're on her team," he chuckled. "She already knows."

The team moved—fast, unified, terrified.

Eight hearts.
One mission.

Bring Celeste home.
Bring the girls home.

■■■i

Celeste jolted awake to faint static in her ear.

"kkkkshhhh—ce… este… hold… tight… we're…
coming—kkhhh"

She froze.

Her chest tightened with relief so sharp it almost hurt.
She pressed a fingertip subtly against her earring,
confirming the connection.

Malik's voice—warped, distant—filtered through again.

"change… position… turn… head…"

Her lungs trembled as she forced a light cough to
confirm the connection.

She closed her eyes for a heartbeat.

"team's… coming….hold…"

They're coming.

She stood straighter than she had in days.

The moment Enrique entered the room, his presence
devoured the space.

"*Todas, a bañarse. Tenemos día ocupado,*" he
announced.
(Everyone, go shower. We've got a busy day.)

Celeste barely heard him over the soft static whispering
inside her ear.

Angela muttered, "*Cabrón…*"
(Asshole.)

He heard.

"What was that?" he barked.

Angela stiffened. "*Nada.*"
(Nothing.)

But his attention shifted to Celeste.

"*You,*" he growled. "*Tú eres el problema.*"
(You're the problem.)

Celeste blinked innocently. "*¿Yo?*"
(Me?)

"The girls are rebelling, *porque crees que mandas*"
(because you think you're in charge.)

She said nothing.

"*Y eso te hace… una amenaza.*"
(And that makes you… a threat.)

He snapped his fingers toward the hallway and exited the room without uttering another word.

"kkksh—we're…coming…"

She nodded.
"I'm ready."

■■■

The situation room buzzed with frantic motion—papers shuffled, weapons were checked, radios clipped, Kevlar secured. But beneath it all sat a heavy, brittle tension strong enough to splinter bone.

Kristian stood at the head of the table, hunched over the digital map projected across the wall, his jaw clenched so tight a muscle jumped in his cheek. Rita and Sebastian flanked him, their eyes scanning satellite overlays, property records, traffic cams—anything that could reinforce Malik's ping.

A vibration rattled across the tabletop.

Rita snatched up her phone and exhaled sharply. "It's Malik. Signal holding."

Kristian turned, hope flickering across his face for the first time in hours. "Where is he?"

Before Rita could answer, the door burst open, and Malik strode in, tablet under one arm, backpack slung over his shoulder, breathless from running up the stairs.

"I'm here," he announced, stepping directly into the center of the clustered team. He held up his tablet, still catching his breath. "Sorry—was downstairs in tech when the signal stabilized. Didn't want to risk losing it again."

Everyone pivoted toward him at once.

"Talk to me," Kristian demanded.

Malik tapped rapidly across the screen. "The pendant's transmitter is intermittent, but it's—barely—coming through. We have audio spikes and… and we have partial video from the pendant's pinhole cam."

The room went silent.

He expanded the feed, cluttered with static and distortion. A glitchy, tilted view appeared—cement walls, rusted shelving, a shadow moving across the frame.

"It's her," Sebastian whispered.

"Celeste," Rita breathed.

Malik continued, voice tight with urgency. "Her earrings are functioning as a low-frequency receiver. I pushed a narrow-band signal through the satellite dish they're using as a jammer—kind of rode the feedback loop. I think she can hear us intermittently—but only when the signal spikes."

"Can she respond?" Kristian asked.

"No," Malik said. "Not verbally. But she moved her head once. She heard me. It was subtle. That's our cue."

He angled the tablet so they all could see as he replayed that moment:
The glitching video showed Celeste's profile in dim light... and when Malik said "Celeste, if you can hear me, turn your head," the feed caught the slightest turn of her head—almost imperceptible, but purposeful.

Kristian braced himself on the table, breathing hard through his nose. "That's enough for me. She's alive. She's listening. We move."

But Malik lifted a hand. "One more thing. She's in motion."

"What?" Sebastian asked.

Malik rotated the tablet. The feed showed jerky movement—shadows passing overhead, girls shifting around her.

"They're about to transport them somewhere. If we don't leave now, we lose her again." Malik swallowed. "Maybe for good."

Kristian turned to the room.
"Gear up. Now. We breach in fifteen."

Rita nodded sharply and jogged toward the lockers. Sebastian followed, slamming a new magazine into his rifle with shaking hands.

Malik tightened the straps of his backpack. "I'll stay linked. I've got enough juice to maintain this connection another hour—hopefully more."

Kristian clapped his shoulder. "Stay with her. Keep talking."

Then he raised his voice, projecting across the room:

"Remember—children are present. No stray rounds. No blind shots. We go in precise."

The team nodded, faces carved with grim determination.

The next moments were a blur of Velcro, metal clicks, rushing footsteps, and Malik's voice through the speakers:

"We're close, Celeste… stay with us."

And for the first time since she vanished, the team felt the crackle of hope.

11

Angela noticed the shift in Celeste before anyone else did.

While the younger girls clustered together in nervous silence—tiny shoulders trembling, fingers woven desperately—the older girl edged closer to Celeste, sensing something in her expression. A heaviness. A decision.

"*Oye*," Angela murmured softly, brushing Celeste's hand with her fingertips. "You good?"

Celeste swallowed hard and nodded, even though the tightness in her chest threatened to crack her ribs open. After a night of terror beneath Enrique's watchful eye, she should've felt numb. Instead, she felt sharper—coiled like a wire stretched too thin.

"*Gracias*, Angie," she whispered, voice thick. "*Por todo*." (Thank you, Angie. For everything.)

Angela's eyes softened. "I meant what I said. When we get out of here, I'm giving you the real deal."

Her lips trembled. "But I need you to stay strong. *¿Sí?*"

Celeste squeezed her hand.

Before she could speak, the door slammed open.

Heavy boots. Harsh voices.

Enrique stepped inside first, cologne poisoning the air, expression carved from stone. Two guards followed, rifles slung carelessly, eyes sweeping the room with practiced cruelty.

"*Arriba*," Enrique barked. "Time to move."
(Get up.)

He tossed black sacks at the girls—head coverings. For transport.

A few gasped. One girl whimpered. Christine clung to Celeste's arm instantly, burying her face against her side.

"Destiny…" Christine whispered, trembling. "*No quiero… por favor…*"
(I don't want to. Please.)

Celeste bent down, cupping the child's cheek. "*Mi amor*, I'm right here. I'm not leaving you."
(My love.)

The girls were lined up. One by one, sacks pulled over their heads. Darkness swallowing vision. Hands forced forward, guided by fists gripping small wrists too tightly.

"But why now?" Angela muttered under her breath, her voice shaking. "*Dios mío*, what are they planning?"
(My God.)

Celeste answered only with a squeeze of her hand—firm, grounding.

A sack dropped over her head.

Smothering darkness. Hot breath trapped inside. The scent of burlap and fear.

She kept Christine pressed close, letting the little girl cling to her shirt.

The march outside was disorienting—rocky dirt beneath their feet, the roar of diesel engines nearby. Voices echoed. Metallic clinks. The screech of a sliding door.

One by one, the girls were lifted into something tall— high steps, cold metal underfoot.

A trailer. A shipping container on wheels.

Celeste felt it immediately.

They were being moved.

Once the entire group was inside, someone ripped the sacks off their heads. Light flooded in from the open doorway— harsh, white, blinding. The interior was bare except for thin metal benches bolted along the walls.

It was colder inside than she expected.

Christine scrambled onto Celeste's lap, wide-eyed, breathing fast like a frightened animal. Angela sat on her other side, her hand searching for Celeste's until their fingers laced together.

More girls sat across from them—some she'd never seen before, all of them pale, exhausted, broken in ways no child should be.

And then her breath caught.

On the far bench, arms wrapped around her knees, head down—

Sonya Friedman.

And next to her, smaller, trembling—

Estelle Gray.

Celeste's stomach twisted. They were alive.

But they were shadows of their photos—thin, hollow, haunted.

The trailer door slammed.

And the lock slid shut.

Darkness swallowed them again, except for a thin strip of light leaking through a cracked seam near the roof.

Celeste inhaled deeply.

This was it.

She couldn't protect all of them from what was coming—but she could prepare them.

"Listen to me," she whispered, voice low but firm. Her arm tightened protectively around Christine. "*Escúchenme, todas.*"
(Listen closely.)

Several girls lifted their heads.
Angela leaned in, sensing the shift.
Sonya's gaze flicked up, confused but hopeful.

"I'm not who you think I am," Celeste murmured. "My name isn't Destiny."

Angela stiffened—but she didn't pull away.

Christine blinked slowly, confused. "Then… who are you?"

Celeste let the words settle in her chest before pushing them out.

"I'm here to help you. All of you. And my team—my people—they're coming."

A gasp rippled through the trailer.

"No way," one girl breathed. "They don't come for us. They never do."

"We've been here too long," another whispered, voice cracking. "Nobody's looking anymore."

Celeste shook her head fiercely. "You're wrong. They are coming. Because I made sure they would. That's why I'm here."

"What are we supposed to do?" Sonya asked, voice soft, shaking.

Celeste scanned their faces, letting her training settle into command mode.

"If we're instructed to get off this trailer, we're going to use the buddy system," she instructed. "Pair up with the girl next to you. No matter what happens, you stay together. You do not separate unless I tell you."

The girls exchanged looks—some scared, others defiant.

Angela nodded first. "It makes sense. They split us easier if we're alone."

Christine tugged Celeste's sleeve. "Who's my buddy?"

Celeste smiled gently. "*Yo, mi amor.* I'm yours."

A few tears slipped down Christine's cheeks, but she nodded bravely.

"Why do we need buddies?" Estelle whispered from across the trailer.

Celeste looked at the scared little girl—barely ten, smaller than Christine, eyes too old for her face.

"Because things are going to move fast. When they open this door, there will be chaos. I need you all low, quiet, and holding onto someone."

One girl frowned. "But you said help is coming."

"It is," Celeste promised. "And when it arrives, I need you to be ready."

The trailer jolted violently as the truck's engine rumbled to life.

Christine grabbed Celeste's shirt.

Angela wrapped an arm around both of them.

And Celeste—hearing the faint crackle of static in her ear—knew Malik was close. Her team was close.

But for these girls?

Time was running out.
Patience was running thin.
Hope was being lost.

***

The trailer lurched again, metal groaning as it hit a pothole. A chorus of sharp breaths rippled through the girls—Christine clutching Celeste's wrist, Angela bracing her other side, the rest holding tight to their partners as instructed.

Celeste swallowed hard, keeping her breathing steady.

'Stay calm. For them.'

A faint static crackled in her ear—so soft she thought she imagined it.

Then it came again.

Sharp. Distinct.
Alive.

"—leste... Ce—ste... if you—hear me... hold—"

Her heart hammered.

"Malik?" she whispered carefully, keeping her voice low but audible.
The girls lifted their heads, confused but silent.

The static cleared like fog burned off by sunlight.

"Carter. I hear you. Loud and clear." Malik's voice shook—not with fear, but with adrenaline and relief. "We've got a visual. Pendant cam stabilized. Feed is clean. I'm relaying your exact location to the squad right now."

Celeste closed her eyes. For the first time since her abduction, she felt something unfamiliar—

Hope.

Celeste kept her face neutral, hiding her shock. She angled her chin down, appearing to comfort Christine as she spoke discreetly toward the pendant.

"Malik, listen carefully," she began, her voice low and controlled. "I count fifteen girls total. Ages range from about seven to sixteen. All alive. Shaken. No injuries that I can see."

Christine squeezed her hand harder. Celeste continued anyway.

"They're scared, Malik. Traumatized. But they're holding on."

A pause.
A breath she didn't know she had been holding.

"Copy that. Sending this to Hudson. Just keep talking. We've got you."

Her throat tightened. She forced herself to stay on the mission.

"We're being transported in a cargo trailer. No restraints. No zip ties. They expect compliance from fear alone."

Angela's gaze flicked toward her, heavy with a question. Celeste squeezed her hand once—an assurance, a plea for silence.

"How many men?" Malik pressed.

"I saw at least four men escort us, armed. Two with rifles. One with a sidearm. One with a baton-looking object."

She lowered her voice further.

"But there may be more at the drop site. Enrique said it would be a 'big day.' I'm guessing that means a transfer or sale."

The word tasted like poison coming out of her mouth.

Malik exhaled sharply. "We're moving fast, Celeste. Team's gearing up. Keep describing the route."

The trailer bounced again, taking a long turn that made several girls lean into Celeste instinctively.

She narrated softly, steadily:

"Road feels unpaved now. We're off the main highway. Heading east—based on the direction of the sun before we loaded. Terrain feels rural, maybe outskirts near the industrial lots."

Malik's keyboard clicks echoed faintly through her earpiece.

"Got it. Cross-referencing the video feed with traffic cams and aerials. You're doing great."

Christine tugged on her sleeve, eyes shining with fear. "Destiny... who are you talking to?"

Celeste placed a gentle hand on her cheek.

"Someone who's going to help us," she whispered.

Angela's breath hitched—she understood more now—but bless her, she stayed quiet.

Celeste turned slightly toward the pendant again.

"One more thing, Malik. I need you to tell the team something important."

"Say it."

"The boss is watching me closely. He's starting to suspect I'm not who I say I am."

Angela stiffened beside her.
The girls leaned closer, seeking security from the only adult who acted like one.

"So, the moment you breach," Celeste continued, "you need to assume I'm compromised. You need to treat me like a civilian—someone who may not be able to fight back."

Malik's voice cracked slightly.
"Celeste... come on."

"Malik," she whispered, feeling Christine curl into her side, "I'm surrounded by children. I can't risk anything."

Silence.
Tense, emotional silence.

"Understood. Relaying now... and Celeste?"
"Yeah?"

"Don't you dare die on us."

Her throat tightened. She forced herself not to cry.

"I'll do my best," she whispered. "Just… hurry."

The trailer hit another bump. Metal rattled.
A few girls whimpered.

Celeste wrapped an arm around Angela and Christine, pulling them close.

"We're going to get out of this," she whispered to them. "All of us."

Angela leaned her forehead against Celeste's, tears trembling at the edges of her lashes.

"If you're lying," she whispered, "I'll find you in the afterlife and haunt you."

Celeste huffed a shaking laugh. "Fair enough."

A transmission came through her earpiece.

"Kristian says hold your position. Team is en route. We're coming, Celeste. Just keep those girls alive."

She straightened her spine despite the fear clawing at it.

"I will."

And for the first time, she believed it.

***

The convoy tore down the empty stretch of highway— three unmarked SUVs slicing through the desert night, red dust billowing behind them. Engines growled. Tires hummed. Every officer inside sat rigid, as if any sudden movement might sever the fragile line connecting Celeste to them.

Malik's voice crackled through the comms.

"Everyone, stand by. Celeste is transmitting. Feed is stable. I repeat—feed is stable."

Kristian slammed his palm against the steering wheel once, a burst of relieved fury. "Fuck—finally."

In the passenger seat, Rita leaned closer to the speaker. "Put her through. Put her through right now."

There was static. And then, Celeste's voice drifted out, thin but steady, carried by miles of desert and a thread of signal.

"—fifteen girls... lowest age looks about seven. No one's hurt badly. We're being moved in a cargo trailer... guards armed with handguns and a shotgun... three confirmed but expect more at the drop point."

Sebastian tightened his grip on the wheel of the second SUV until his knuckles were almost popping out of his hand. He'd heard Celeste speak a thousand times, but never like this—measured, deliberate, and calm because she had to be.

Kristian exhaled shakily. "I still can't believe she's alive," he whispered. "She's fucking alive."

"Quiet," Rita snapped softly—not harsh, but desperate. "Let her talk."

Celeste continued, voice wavering only once.

"The girls are terrified, but they're holding together. I... I told them to stay low. Buddy up. No sudden movements. They're trusting me. Don't make them regret it."

Sebastian bowed his head, eyes burning.
"Jesus, Cel."

Malik's voice cut in again, breathless with urgency. "Her pendant camera is active. Feed's shaky, but usable. We've got location tracking locked. They're heading east—toward the outer lots near the interstate. Possibly a container yard."

Kristian straightened, eyes sharpening.
"Copy. Everyone, stay tight."

Rita swallowed hard, staring out the windshield into the blur of streetlights.
Hearing Celeste—not just her voice, but her resolve— hit her like a punch.

She wasn't broken. She wasn't giving up. She was fighting, even while trapped.

Malik's voice cracked suddenly. "She's talking again."

Celeste's voice returned, softer this time—almost a whisper.

"I don't know what's coming when we stop… but whatever it is… please hurry and meet us there."

Kristian closed his eyes for half a second, letting the words land squarely on his heart.

Then he opened them with fire.

"Hang on, Carter," he said into the radio, his voice firm, unshakeable. "We're coming for you. I don't care who stands in the way—we're going to bring you and those girls home."

The radios echoed with the quiet rumble of agreement from every SUV.

Focused.
Furious.
Determined.

Their deputy had just handed them a lifeline.

And now they were going to war.

12

The semi-truck rumbled through the final stretch of desert road, headlights cutting through the darkness like blunt blades. Dust churned beneath its wheels, rising in thick clouds that disappeared into the cold night air. Inside the sealed trailer, the girls jolted with each uneven bump, some whimpering, some whispering prayers under their breath. Christine clung to Celeste's arm the entire ride, her small body trembling against the deputy's side.

Celeste bent down toward her. "It's okay, baby. I'm right here."

But even she didn't believe her own words—not entirely.

The truck slowed, then hissed as air brakes released. A hollow metallic echo reverberated around them as the vehicle rolled across the uneven gravel of the container yard. It felt like entering another world—one where nobody screamed, nobody questioned, nobody lived unless allowed to.

The engine shut off.

Silence hit like a punch.

No birds. No distant cars. No humans besides the men outside. Just desert wind slipping between rusty metal walls.

Celeste placed one steadying hand on Angela's thigh and squeezed. Angela nodded, trying to look brave for the younger girls even as fear hollowed her eyes.

Outside, dozens of boots approached the truck—crisp, heavy, synchronized. Not frantic. Not careless.

Trained.

Celeste swallowed hard. Cartel-level organization. Military-grade discipline.

She closed her eyes and prayed Malik was still with her.
Prayed the team was near.
Prayed she could buy these girls enough time.

***

The yard stretched out in rows and labyrinths of old shipping containers, each one rusting beneath flickering floodlights perched on tall metal poles. Silhouettes moved between them—armed guards wearing tactical vests, radios clipped to their shoulders, and rifles that gleamed under the harsh lights.

This was not a makeshift operation. This was an infrastructure. A polished machine built on stolen children.

Enrique stepped out of the back seat of a black SUV, stretching his neck and inhaling the cool desert air like he owned the night itself. His swagger returned instantly—chin up, shoulders loose, eyes sweeping the yard with confidence he hadn't earned.

Pablo emerged from the passenger seat of another truck, built like he'd been carved from brick. Tattoos covered his forearms and crept up his neck. He flicked ash from a cigarette without bothering to look where it landed.

And behind them walked a man Celeste had only heard about from Angela—a tall, severe-looking figure dressed in dark clothes and expensive boots.

Reynaldo *'El Pesado'* Méndez.
The money man. The handler. The muscle.
The cartel's middleman for human cargo.

Guards parted as he approached. His presence radiated command.

He called out, *"llegaron temprano. Eso me gusta."*
(You arrived early. I like that.)

Enrique smirked. *"Claro. Somos profesionales, ¿no?"*
(Of course. We're professionals, right?)

Two guards rolled forward heavy suitcases and placed them at Pablo's feet. He crouched, opened the first case, and paused.

Neat stacks of cash filled the entire frame—bundles wrapped tightly, each stamped and dated. Pablo lifted a stack, fanned it out, and brought it close to his nose.

"Huele a dinero bien ganado," he said, smiling wide.
(Smells like hard-earned money.)

The guards chuckled.

Reynaldo didn't. His impatience radiated off him in waves.

"Órale pues, ya enseñaron el dinero. Ahora enséñame el producto."
(Alright then, you got the money. Now show me the product.)

He motioned toward the trailer.

Enrique moved forward, hand on the latch—

But headlights suddenly illuminated the yard.

Three sets. Low. Controlled. Approaching quickly.

Pablo's smile dropped.
Guards shifted instantly into position, rifles raised and pointed outward.

Reynaldo spun around, squinting.

"*¿Quiénes chingados son esos?*"
(Who the fuck are they?)

The guards murmured among themselves—quick, nervous exchanges. No one knew. No one expected company. No one had leaked intel.

Enrique's hand crept toward his weapon.

Reynaldo barked to his men, "*Quietos.*"
(Hold.)

But Pablo was spiraling, rage overtaking logic as he rounded on the guards.

"*¡Hijos de putas! Ustedes nos vendieron. ¡Nos pusieron una trampa!*" he roared.
(Sons of bitches. You sold us out! You set us up!)

The guards pointed their rifles at him.
He pointed his at them.

Seconds from chaos.

■■■

Malik's voice crackled through the radio:

"Confirmation—Celeste is in the trailer. I repeat: she is in the trailer. Fifteen minors total. Armed men outside. Proceed with extreme caution."

Kristian breathed out hard, eyes fixed on the glow of floodlights beyond the barriers.

There was no room for emotion.
Not anymore.

"Positions!" he snapped.

The team scattered into formation—silent, precise, lethal when needed.

Sebastian peeked from behind the container wall.
"Multiple hostiles. Long guns. At least a dozen visible."

Rita whispered, "Do we have an angle?"

Kristian clenched his jaw.
"We do now."

Alfred signaled with two fingers—perimeter guards shifting away. An opening.

Kristian gave a single nod.

The breach was on.

***

Inside the dark cargo trailer, the girls huddled close, breaths shaky, little hands clutching Celeste's clothes like she was the last solid thing in a collapsing world. The metal walls throbbed with every muffled shout outside—Spanish curses, frantic footsteps, the metallic clack of weapons being loaded.

The air felt too tight. Too hot. Too still.

Celeste forced herself to breathe evenly, though her heart hammered hard enough to bruise her ribs.

Angela whispered, "Destiny… *¿qué está pasando?*"
(What's happening?)

Celeste shook her head once— small, controlled.
"It's okay. Just noise. Stay close."

But she knew it wasn't 'just noise'.
The tone of the voices had changed— sharper, panicked, fractured.

And then—
A familiar voice boomed across the yard, distorted through the trailer walls but unmistakable.

"Las Vegas police, drop your weapons!"

Celeste's blood froze.

Kristian. It was Kristian.

He was here.

But that meant—
Gunfire wasn't just possible. It was inevitable.

The girls all jerked toward the sound. A few cried out.

Christine's tiny fingers dug into Celeste's wrist, right where her mother's bracelet hugged her skin. Christine's eyes widened, recognition slamming into her.

"*La pulsera…*" she whispered.
(The bracelet.)

Celeste cupped Christine's cheek quickly.
"Later, *mi amor*. Hold on to Angela, *¿sí?*"
(Okay?)

Christine shook her head violently. "No! I want to stay with you!"

Celeste pressed her forehead to Christine's. "Listen. You're brave. You're strong. I need you to help Angela protect the others."

Her voice trembled—but she didn't let it break.

"Now go."

Christine hesitated, lower lip trembling... then she nodded and crawled back toward Angela, clutching the bracelet one last time before letting go.

Celeste exhaled shakily.

***

Through the metal walls, Celeste could hear Kristian shouting commands:

"Last chance, drop the weapons!"

Then Reynaldo shouted something back—furious, unintelligible over the trailer's echo.

Boots scraped. Rifles shifted.
The world outside teetered on the edge of gunfire.

Celeste gestured frantically to the girls.

"¡Todas al piso! ¡Ahora!"
(Everyone get down! Now!)

Small bodies flattened against the trailer floor. Some cried silently. Some whimpered into each other's clothes.

Celeste scanned the interior—no cover, no shield, nowhere safe.

She crouched low herself, inching toward the door with careful, deliberate movements. Every instinct screamed to stay back—but she needed intel. Direction. Preparation.

She pressed her ear to the cold metal.

Men shouted.
Footsteps scattered.
Then Enrique's enraged, unmistakable voice.
"¡Pendejos! ¡Escóndanse! ¡Nos cayeron!"
(Idiots! Take cover! They're onto us!)

His next words were lower, breathless, venomous.

"Lo sabía… lo juro por Dios… lo sabía."
(I knew it… I swear to God… I knew it.)

Celeste's stomach dropped.

He suspected.
Not fully.
But enough.

***

POW!

A gunshot tore through the night, echoing inside the trailer so violently that several girls screamed and covered their ears.

Another shot. Then another. Automatic fire erupted— rapid, vicious, thunderous.

The trailer shuddered as stray rounds hit the exterior, pinging off the metal like hail amplified a hundred times.

Christine screamed, "Destiny!"

Celeste whipped around.
"Angela—¡agarra a Christine!"
(Grab Christine!)

Angela dragged the trembling child beneath her arms, pulling two smaller girls in with her.

Celeste raised her voice over the gunfire.

"Stay down! Don't move unless I say!"

Her voice shook but held strong.

Bullets slapped against the trailer walls.
Men outside yelled.
Radios crackled.
Boots stampeded across gravel.

The entire structure felt alive with chaos.

Celeste crawled forward again—each movement deliberate, low, controlled. The smell of rust and dust filled her lungs.

***

The gunfire outside rattled the trailer like a living thing. Every burst made the metal vibrate; every echo seemed to ricochet through the girls' bones. Some cried openly now; others tried to cover their cries with their arms.

Celeste whispered urgently, "Stay down. *No levanten la cabeza*. Don't move unless I say."
(Keep your heads down.)

She crawled forward, inch by inch, toward the door— trying to gauge distance, numbers, survival.

Outside—Spanish curses tore through the chaos.

"*¡Cuiden los camiones!*"
(Protect the trucks!)

"*¡No dejen que pasen!*"
(Don't let them get through!)

Boots pounded past. Bodies hit the sand. Automatic rifle bursts rattled the air.

Then she heard him. Enrique.

His voice cut through the firefight like a serrated blade.

"¡*Pablo!* ¡*Nos vendieron, cabrón! Te dije que algo olía mal con esta entrega!*"
(Pablo! They sold us out, bastard! I told you something smelled off with this delivery!)

He was furious—furious enough that Celeste felt the temperature in the trailer drop.

A heavy boot stepped directly in front of the door.

Another step.

The latch turned.

Every girl gasped at once.

The door swung open, blinding light flooding in. The silhouette standing there was unmistakable: broad shoulders, rifle slung over his arm, jaw clenched like cracked stone.

Enrique's eyes burned into the darkness.

He saw Celeste and he smiled.

Not kindly. Not amused. But knowingly.

"*Lo sabía… algo de ti nunca cuadró.*"
(I knew it… something about you never added up.)

He raised his arm—not to fire, but to grab.

Before Celeste could retreat, his hand shot forward, clamping around her arm like iron.

She twisted—
He yanked—
She stumbled into him.

Gasps rose behind her—Angela, Christine, the girls watched helplessly.

"Let go of me," Celeste hissed.

Enrique leaned close, voice low and venomous.
"*Tú vienes conmigo.*"
(You're coming with me.)

With one brutal jerk, he dragged her fully out of the trailer, slamming the door behind her.

"DESTINY!" Christine screamed inside.

Celeste's heart cracked—but Enrique's grip only tightened as he shoved her forward through the sand.

The firefight screeched to a sudden halt.

Enrique's voice boomed across the yard:

"*¡Alto!* Everybody stop!"

He dragged Celeste out into the open, one arm locked around her throat, the muzzle of his pistol wedged near her ribs.
For the first time since she was taken, the team saw Celeste.
Clothes ripped. Face dirty. Hair messy—Celeste looked exhausted.
Rita swore under her breath. Sebastian's knuckles were on full display around his weapon.

Kristian's team ducked behind overturned crates and rusted excavators. Dozens of guards lay scattered—some down, some wounded. Only a handful of men remained standing on the cartel's side: Enrique, Pablo, Reynaldo, and a couple of guards—one in particular was a jittery guard who was clutching his rifle too hard.

Kristian emerged from behind a truck, rifle strapped around his body and a pistol in his hand. He gripped it tightly.

"Let her go!" he shouted.

Enrique laughed—a wild, strained bark.

"¿Soltarla? Debes estar loco. Tengo lo que quieres, y esta perra es eso!"
(Let her go? You must be crazy. I got what you want, and this bitch is it.)

He shoved Celeste forward, displaying her like a bargaining chip.

Pablo narrowed his eyes. *"¿Quién carajos es ella?"*
(Who the fuck is she?)

Enrique's voice cracked with triumph.

"¡La policía!"
(The police!)

Kristian's jaw locked into place.

Enrique raised his voice to the unit across the yard.

"You want her back? Then you let us walk away. Clear path. No shots. We go; she lives!"

Behind the trailer door, Christine's cries had hit a breaking point—shrill, panicked.

She pounded on the inside wall.

And then—
Her voice cracked through the chaos: "Officer Destiny!"

Time froze.

Pablo stiffened. Reynaldo's eyes widened. Enrique's grip faltered for a fraction of a second.

The eyes shifted towards the trailer, and Celeste could tell.

Celeste felt the smallest opening. She took it.

With every ounce of force she had left, she slammed her elbow backward—straight into Enrique's ribcage.

The air rushed out of him. He stumbled and lost his grip on Celeste.

Kristian moved before anyone else could.

One fluid step.
One raised pistol.
One breath.

POW.

The shot echoed like a hammer.

Enrique's eyes went wide, then empty. Enrique's body hit the sand with a heavy, final thud.

For one fractured second, the entire yard fell into stunned silence.

Celeste stood frozen where he'd held her moments earlier—her chest heaving, lungs burning, ears ringing. The desert air felt razor sharp against her skin.

'He's dead. Kristian shot him.'

Behind her, the trailer exploded with terrified screams.

"Destiny! Destiny!"

"¡Destiny! ¡Regresa!"
(Destiny! Come back!)

And Christine—her voice cutting through everything like a blade:

"Officer Destiny!"

Kristian's heart lurched as the words carried across the yard. Even amidst the chaos, hearing the title attached to her undercover name nearly broke him.

But there was no time to feel it.

Pablo shouted something guttural in Spanish, grabbing his rifle and moving behind the stack of shipping containers where Reynaldo and the guard stood.

"*¡Mueve el camión!*"
(Move the truck!)

The jittery guard ran toward the trailer latch to ensure it was secure, fumbling with trembling hands.

Sebastian spotted him and fired a warning shot—purposeful, angled, cracking the dirt directly beside the man's boot.

"Back away from that trailer!"

The guard startled so violently that he dropped his rifle.

Kristian surged forward, his voice a roar:

"Move in! Move in!"

The team stormed the yard with precision drills—tactical, disciplined, and unstoppable. Sand flew under their boots as they advanced, using rusted earthmovers and stacked containers for cover.

Gunfire erupted again—this time tightly controlled, strategic.

Pablo barked orders while Reynaldo shouted over him.

"*¡Protéjan los bienes! ¡Llegan los federales!*"

(Protect the merchandise! The feds are here!)

"*No los federales, idiota—¡la policía local!*"
(Not the feds, idiot—local cops!)

They were panicking.
Their chain of command dissolving.
This wasn't part of their plan.

And Celeste knew it. She could feel it in the air—the fracture, the shift.

She stumbled backward toward the trailer, adrenaline pushing her legs even when her body wanted to collapse. She reached the door, hands shaking as she dragged it open.

The girls were still crouched low, clinging to each other—terrified, sobbing, trembling.

Christine launched at her instantly, arms tight around her waist. Celeste pulled the door to the trailer shut—mostly—to protect the girls. She knelt down.

"*¡No me dejes!*" Christine cried.
(Don't leave me!)

Celeste cupped her face urgently.
"Shh, shh. I'm right here, baby. I'm right here."

Angela grabbed Celeste's shirt with trembling fingers. "Destiny—*¿qué hacemos?* What do we do?"

Celeste inhaled sharply, her training outshouting her fear.

"Listen to me. Everyone stays low. No standing. No running. Stay in the trailer. It's safer than the open yard. Do you understand?"

Some nodded vigorously. Others cried too hard to answer.

Christine clung tighter. "*¿Y tú?*"

Celeste pressed her forehead to the child's. "I'll be right here. I promise."

***

Rita's voice crackled through her radio as she fired twice in Pablo's direction.

"They're pinned at the far containers—east section!"

"Copy," Kristian replied, moving around the front of the semi-truck.

Sebastian slid next to him, reloading quickly. "Trailer is secure! Carter has the kids!"

Kristian exhaled shakily—the closest thing to relief he'd felt since Celeste disappeared. "We hold this line. Nobody gets near that trailer."

Pablo peeked around a container and fired erratically—he was losing control—losing confidence.

Reynaldo shouted at him, "*¡Regruparse! ¡A la parte trasera!*"
(Regroup! To the back!)

But Pablo shook his head wildly.
"*¡Estamos jodidos!*"
(We're screwed!)

Sebastian leaned toward Kristian. "They're cracking."

Kristian's knuckles tightened on his rifle.

"Good. Keep the pressure."

***

Inside the trailer, Celeste positioned herself at the threshold—half-inside, half-exposed—forming a barrier between gunfire and children.

The pendant camera flickered, sending a jerky feed back to Malik.

Malik's voice crackled faintly in her earpiece:
"Celeste, I'm getting everything. The team is closing in on the trailer. Basing what I'm seeing from Kristian's body cam, they're keeping the men from approaching. Keep doing what you're doing."

Her throat tightened with emotion she didn't have time to feel.

Angela tugged her arm. "Destiny... *tienes sangre*."
(Destiny... you're bleeding.)

Celeste glanced down—she hadn't noticed the graze on her forearm.

"I'm okay," she lied. "Go back with Christine. Keep her head down."

Christine sobbed into Angela's shoulder.

***

Reynaldo realized the police were flanking them. He cursed under his breath.

"*Pablo—llévate a las chicas! ¡Usa el tráiler como escudo!*"
(Pablo—take the girls! Use the trailer as a shield!)

Pablo darted toward the cab of the semi-truck, firing wildly to cover his movement.

Kristian aimed carefully.

"Ortega—tires. Now."

Sebastian fired two perfect shots.

The truck's front tires burst, collapsing under the weight of the cab.

Pablo swore violently.
"¡Hijo de puta!"
(Son of a bitch!)

Now the truck wasn't going anywhere.

And Celeste's girls weren't going anywhere either.

Reynaldo lunged from behind the containers, firing at Rita and Maria. Kristian swung around the grill of a forklift and dropped into a kneeling stance—precision perfect.

He waited for the shot—
Waited for Reynaldo to expose enough—

POW.

Reynaldo fell to his knees, blood blooming across his chest.

"Target down," Kristian murmured.

Pablo let out a choked, furious cry.

He lifted his rifle, aiming at the trailer—
Aimed at the children—
At Celeste—

"No!" Rita yelled.

But Pablo never got the shot off. Sebastian fired once.

Pablo collapsed backward, rifle clattering onto the sand.

Celeste flinched as Pablo fell, instinctively shielding the girls with her body.

Christine peeked over Angela's arm. "Is it over?"

Celeste swallowed a sob.

"Yard is secure," Kristian spoke over the radio, as though he was answering Christine's question.

"It's over, *mi amor*."

Celeste slowly opened the trailer, allowing the remaining sunlight to flow onto the girls.

She scanned the yard—Kristian's silhouette emerging through drifting sand, rifle lowered, eyes locked on her like he was afraid she might vanish again.

Emotion slammed into her chest so hard her knees nearly buckled.

He reached her first.

"Celeste…"
Her name left him like a prayer.

Before she could respond, small hands tugged her shirt—children crying and shaking.

The sight shattered something inside her.

She dropped to her knees and wrapped them all in her arms, tears finally slipping free.

"We've got you," she whispered. "You're safe. You're safe now."

Christine pressed her face into Celeste's neck.
"Thank you."

Celeste hugged her tighter.

Kristian turned away briefly, wiping at his eyes before barking over the radio:

"All units—Start medical. We've got them. We got the girls."

And for the first time in months—
For the first time since the disappearances began—

Hope didn't feel like a lie.

13

Gun smoke still clung to the air like a ghost when the last echoes of gunfire finally faded into silence.

The container yard—moments ago a battlefield—was now flooded with flashing red and blue lights, paramedics weaving between officers, stretchers being unfolded, radios crackling with frantic orders.

Celeste's body shook uncontrollably. Her breath hitched in sharp, painful bursts. The dry desert wind stung her eyes, but it wasn't the wind making them water—it was everything she'd held together for days suddenly buckling at once.

Beside her, the girls crowded around her legs, refusing to leave the safety of her shadow, regardless of seeing the numerous officers and paramedics. Their fingers wrapped around her pants, her shirt, her arms. Tiny hands. Trembling hands. Hands that had learned to cling to anything steady in a world that had offered them none.

Celeste rose to her feet and faced Kristian.

He stepped towards her, chest rising and falling in violent relief. When he reached her, he didn't slow—he grabbed her, pulling her against him, hugging her so fiercely that for the first time since she'd gone under, Celeste let her knees give out.

She collapsed into him, a broken sob ripping up her throat.

He caught her before she hit the ground. The girls pressed in as well, supporting her in whatever small ways they could.

Sebastian and Rita rushed in, each gripping an arm, a shoulder, bracing her trembling frame.

"You're okay... you're okay..." Sebastian whispered, although it was his voice that shook.

Rita brushed Celeste's hair back with trembling fingers, eyes shining with unbearable relief. "We thought we lost you," she choked out.

Celeste couldn't speak. She pressed her forehead into Kristian's shoulder as tears poured freely—hot, breath-stealing, unstoppable.

But the girls...

The girls didn't let go.

As soon as Celeste was lowered to a kneel, Christine wrapped both arms around her waist from behind, sobbing into her back. Angela dropped beside her, looping her arms around Celeste's shoulders. The younger girls continued to crowd her, clinging to her like she was the last solid thing in the world.

"*No nos dejes*... please don't leave us..."
"You kept your word." The girl who once had doubts about help coming, was in shock.

Their cries blended with sirens, with radios, with the wind—the sound of trauma breaking open, pouring out.

Celeste gathered them all into her arms, shaking so hard she could barely hold herself up.

"My sweet girls," she whispered through sobs.
"You're safe now. I swear, it's over."

Angela pressed her forehead to Celeste's temple, crying quietly. *"Gracias… por no rendirte… por volver por nosotras…"*
(Thank you… for not giving up… for coming back for us.)

Celeste pulled her closer, holding her as though she would never allow anyone to take her again.

***

Screeching tires.
Doors thrown open.
A stampede of footsteps.

Families rushed toward the yard, the sight of their children sending them into emotional freefall.

Screams of joy. Sobs of disbelief.
Parents collapsing to their knees as they embraced daughters they feared they would never see again.

Every reunion tore another piece from Celeste's heart.

But Christine—Christine watched the chaos unfold with wide, hopeful eyes… until hope slowly drained from her face.

She saw Estelle with her grandmother.
Sonya with her mother.
Angela was comforting a girl who'd found her aunt.

But no one ran for Christine.

No one called her name.

No one reached out for her.

Her small body sank further into Celeste's side, trembling.

Celeste cupped Christine's cheek, brushing away a tear. "I see it," she whispered. "I know."

Then—Leticia Holland came stumbling into the clearing, mascara streaked, hair wild, hysteria twisting her face. Nico trailed behind her, tugging at his sleeves, eyes darting as if searching for an exit.

"Christine—*mi bebé*—"
(My baby.)

Christine recoiled instantly, shrinking back until she was pressed against Celeste's legs. She slipped behind her, fingers fisting in Celeste's shirt, gripping so hard her knuckles turned white.

Celeste felt it—the fear. The instinctive recoil.

Rita took a sharp step forward. "Carter—"

The Hollands turned pale upon seeing Rita. She refused to make eye contact.

Celeste didn't turn, but her posture shifted, her attention narrowing. "Gaines."

Just her name. Quiet. Firm.

Rita stopped. Jaw tight, eyes burning, she leaned in close enough that only Celeste could hear her.

"She's afraid of them," Rita said under her breath. "And there's a reason. Her father sold her. He made the deal."

Celeste's expression changed—not shock, but clarity. Pieces snapping together. The fear. The hiding. The grip that hadn't loosened.

Slowly, deliberately, Celeste straightened and stepped forward, placing herself fully between Christine and her parents.

Leticia staggered closer. "Please—please let me hold my baby—"

"Don't touch her," Celeste said, her voice steady but carrying unmistakable authority.

It was not a shout. It was not loud.

But it froze the entire yard.

Nico swallowed hard. "We—we're her parents—"

"You sold her," Rita spoke, soft but firm.

Leticia shook her head violently, breath coming too fast, hands fluttering uselessly at her chest. "I didn't—I didn't know!"

Celeste stepped forward, her expression unreadable, her voice cutting through the clearing.

"You chose not to know," she said. Then she turned to Nico, her gaze locking onto him. "And you—" She pointed. "You sold your own daughter. For whatever excuse you told yourself. Do you know what these girls went through? And you *willingly* put her through that," her voice cracked. She cleared her throat.

Leticia staggered back a step, knees buckling. "No—no, that's not—" Her words collapsed into a strangled sob as she clawed at the air, shaking her head harder, as if denial alone might undo it.

Nico crumpled, dropping to his knees as sobs tore out of him. "No—please—please—"

Christine cried harder, burying her face against Celeste's stomach.

Celeste immediately drew her closer, stroking her hair. Her voice softened—only for her. "I won't let anyone hurt you again."

Christine nodded into her shirt—shaking, broken... but trusting. Completely trusting.

Celeste lifted her head.

"Officer Ortega."

He stepped forward without hesitation.

"I don't know how he managed to leave the station," Celeste said evenly, "but arrest him. Full charges. Human trafficking. Sale of a child. Endangerment. Everything."

Sebastian moved in. Nico screamed as the cuffs closed around his wrists, his pleas dissolving into incoherent begging.

Leticia surged forward, panic spilling over into desperation. "Christine, please—I'm your mother—" Her hands trembled, reaching, grasping for something—anything—as her voice broke completely.

Celeste turned on her.

One look—sharp, absolute—made Leticia freeze mid-step, the fight draining out of her like air from a punctured lung.

"Officer Gaines," Celeste said, her tone calm but final, "escort Mrs. Holland to the station. She has a great deal to answer for."

Her gaze dropped briefly to the bracelet on her wrist. Celeste reached out, removed it, and let it fall at Leticia's feet.

"Take that with you."

Leticia stares at the bracelet as it falls to the sand. She tried to reach Christine one last time.
Christine turned away.

Celeste shielded her with her entire body.

Once Nico was driven away and Leticia was escorted off, the paramedics approached Celeste.

They urged her to sit on the gurney. She didn't fight it.

Her limbs were dead weight, she needed to have her arm assessed, and her muscles were spasming beneath her bruises. Her breathing stuttered.

Christine climbed into her lap again, curling against her chest as though she belonged there.

Angela sat on the gurney beside them, leaning her head on Celeste's shoulder.

Celeste's throat tightened.

"You're both safe," she murmured. "I'll keep you safe."

Christine lifted her head but didn't utter a word.
Celeste looked at Christine's wide eyes.
Once heavy eyes were now full of hope. Eyes that were once searching for comfort were clearly comforted.

Celeste looked at the sea of reunions around them, then down at the child clutching her with shaking fingers.

"Christine," she whispered, brushing her thumb along the girl's cheek, "would you like to come with me tonight?"

Christine blinked, surprised. "To your house? Like a sleepover?"

Celeste nodded and chuckled. "We can start there. After everything you've been through… you deserve somewhere gentle. Somewhere safe. Somewhere you're loved."

Christine burst into tears—not from fear, not from trauma—but from relief so overwhelming, it cracked something open inside her.

"*Por favor,*" she whispered. "*Por favor….no me dejes sola.*"
(Please. Please don't leave me by myself.)

Celeste hugged her so tightly her arms trembled. "Never," she promised. "You're not alone anymore."

Angela wiped her eyes and touched Celeste's arm. "*¿Puedo ir contigo también? Solo por un tiempo.*"
(Can I come with you, too? Just for a while.)

Celeste took her hand.

"*Sí, mi amor. Hasta que estés lista.*"
(Yes, sweetheart. Until you're ready.)

And for the first time since she'd been taken, Celeste allowed herself to inhale fully.

The girls were alive.

They were safe.

And the nightmare was over.

She leaned into Kristian's steady hands, felt Rita's arm around her back, heard Sebastian's ragged exhale beside her—

And at last, Celeste Carter let her body collapse into the arms of the family that had fought like hell to bring her home.

They hadn't saved them all—they wished they had—but saving these girls meant the world wasn't lost yet. It meant there was still something worth fighting for.

www.ingramcontent.com/pod-product-compliance
Lightning Source LLC
Chambersburg PA
CBHW020845260626
47169CB00003B/1145